Printed in the United States of America

Publisher: WarFox Publications
Cover Design: Dylan Vigil

Library of Congress Cataloging-in-Publication Data

Library of Congress Control Number: 2018938771

Rohrbacher, Gunnar.
      The Funniest Scenes in the World, Volume 2 /
by Gunnar Rohrbacher.

      ISBN 978-0-9982884-1-3

WarFox Publications LLC is a registered trademark.

10 9 8 7 6 5 4 3 2 1

About the Author

Gunnar Todd Rohrbacher is the Artistic Director of Actors Comedy Studio (ACS) and one of Hollywood's best-known acting coaches. He is also a highly regarded writer, director, producer and actor within Hollywood's comedy scene, earning acclaim and rave reviews for more than 20 years.

He's an Expert Contributor to Backstage and has produced and directed dozens of shows of all kinds, including improv, sketch, actor's showcases, plays and one-person shows. Gunnar was trained and mentored by some of the industry's most respected comedy authorities including Lisa Kudrow, Cynthia Szigeti, Phyllis Katz and many others.

As an actor (SAG-AFTRA), Gunnar starred in two pilots for NBC; Prime Time Comedy, produced by the famed George Schlatter of *Laugh-In* and the semi-improvised sitcom, *The Weekend*.

Before launching Actors Comedy Studio, Gunnar spent a decade teaching on-camera audition technique classes in multiple venues throughout Los Angeles. Prior to teaching TV & film acting, Gunnar taught improvisation and sketch writing for an additional ten years. With virtually every aspect of comedic instruction under his belt, Gunnar carved a niche for himself in LA's vast teaching landscape as the "go to" on-camera comedy coach.

Gunnar is an alumnus of the acclaimed ACME Comedy Theater in Hollywood, where he was a member of the Main Company. He taught all levels of improv, beginning through advanced for many years. In addition, Gunnar created and taught sketch writing courses and directed the school's performance labs. He was also the Director of ACME's Sunday Company of up and coming talent.

In addition, Gunnar designed and exclusively taught the Acting for Animators program for Walt Disney Animation Studios and was a character consultant on two animated Disney features, *Meet The Robinsons* and *Bolt*. He introduced Acting for Sitcoms to the curriculum of both the New York Film Academy and the American Academy of Dramatic Arts.

He continues to teach performance and writing workshops at various comedy festivals and private acting studios around the country. Of note, he's been a guest instructor at the SAG Conservatory, The Groundlings, CalArts, LAComedyFest and Act Now Studio in Portland, Oregon, Film Base, Dublin, Ireland.

A Note from Gunnar

Hi, everyone! I hope you enjoyed The Funniest Scenes in the World, Volume 1 and found them useful. Volume 2 features 25 brand new, additional scenes formatted in the exact same way.

As I said in the opening pages of Volume 1, these scenes are very special to me and I'm grateful to have the opportunity to share them with fellow actors. I had fun writing them and my wish is that they bring more fun into the world. If you own Volume 1, you already know the drill. If, for some reason, you're starting with Volume 2, read on to discover how to use these books to your greatest advantage.

I'm excited to introduce a valuable tool into the marketplace that I think is badly needed: a book of original scenes that are worthy of being performed for agents, managers, casting directors and network executives. A book of scenes that are worthy of being shot and broadcast on television and are formatted like proper scripts used by professional actors. I'm proud to say; you're reading that book.

That would be a very bold assertion if it had not been tested. Fortunately, it has!

I'm in a rather unique position. I am a writer, actor, director, producer and teacher who happens to also own an acting studio, Actors Comedy Studio in Los Angeles. We primarily teach acting and audition technique for on-camera comedy; sitcoms, half-hours, dramedies, whatever term you like. We also offer writing and singing classes. Of note, we do two other things at ACS that are relevant to this collection of scenes. We host casting director workshops and produce student showcases.

Many of the scenes in this book have been performed live in one configuration or another. A few are brand spanking new. Within casting director workshops, actors will perform scenes from television pilots that never aired, scenes from television that have aired and at ACS scenes I have written.

Time and again, these scenes have grabbed the attention of our guest casting directors. They love them and are often curious where the actors found them. They're amused, surprised and impressed when they hear they came from me, their teacher. A few have asked if they can add my work to their portfolio of scenes they take with them to other venues.

We also produce actor's showcases at ACS, and again, the writing has stood out as exemplary. Agents, managers and network executives have all asked after our industry showcases, "Where did you get all that material?" When I say I wrote it, I'm often met with a look of complete disbelief. Then a flood of compliments that every scene worked, every actor was properly cast and there was diversity and variety within the tone of the scenes.

None of this is to boast. I simply think if you're going to lay down some hard-earned money for this book, you should have some context. I love writing short scenes more than any kind of writing. I have a knack for it.

It's trickier than you might think to write a scene that has a beginning, middle and end, unique characters in familiar situations, is equally weighted for both actors, has some relatability to our current culture and wraps up in four to six pages. In all of these scenes, it's easy to identify who the characters are, where they are and what they're doing with several laughs per page.

So while my work has had validation from a wide swath of industry professionals, these scenes are new in the scheme of things. They aren't from existing works. They have not been done over and over again. They aren't scenes from plays from the 1950s or movies from the 1980s. Don't get me wrong. I love the classics, but actors deserve a better choice than dated material that, more often than not, features an indelible performance by a notable actor.

These scenes are designed to make you the star. I hope they do.

Acknowledgments

Putting this collection of scenes together was a labor of love and I did not do it alone. Here is where I make a full and complete confession: it wasn't even my idea. Fortunately, I business married well. Lauren Marie Bertoni is the co-owner of Actors Comedy Studio and a very well-educated and accomplished teacher in her own right.

This particular light bulb went off over her head and she's done an incredible amount of work to make this published collection a reality. Thank you, Lauren. Joining forces with you is the best decision I've ever made, hands down.

Dylan Vigil created the cover, which makes me smile every time I see it. He's a badass, ninja warrior graphic designer and did an excellent job making this book look good.

Gail Borges, Sarah McLean, Thomas Ochoa, Nicole Serrat and Dan Kacvinski also made a significant contribution to this collection. Thanks!

I also want to express gratitude to my students and the amazing community that populates Actors Comedy Studio. The people who come here are special and supportive in a way that I think is quite rare. I do my best to offer all my skills and knowledge freely as a teacher. In turn, they challenge me to grow and inspire me to continue dreaming.

Walking into a classroom makes me happy even on my worst days. I'm grateful I've been given the opportunity and am perpetually humbled that people come to me with their hopes and dreams in tow. Thanks to all the artists who make themselves vulnerable to my notes, direction and playfully sarcastic jabs to "take it up a notch." Let's be champions of light, love and laughter in this world together.

How to Use This Book

Here is some help on how to get the best bang for your buck with this book. The format is pretty simple. The scenes are organized into the following categories: male/female, female/female, male/male and gender-neutral. The gender-neutral scenes are also age neutral. Thus, each traditional category is made larger by the additional scenes that most anyone can perform.

Watch Some Examples

In addition, the scenes were all envisioned for the screen rather than stage. Some of them have been shot and produced and are viewable as MiniComs™ on our production site, ACSDigital.tv. Not all of the scenes in this book are represented there, but if you'd like to see some that were shot live in front of a studio audience (the laughter is real), with rehearsal, direction and terrific actors, please check them out. Even if your scene of choice is not one that we shot for our two seasons of MiniComs™, you might get some ideas about performance energy, timing, rhythm, pace, delivery, etc.

Some scenes may seem broader than others. Some may read more poignant to you. That was intentional. There is a wide range of comedy being distributed by an enormous number of broadcasters and streaming services. With all the comedy shows being produced for ABC, CBS, NBC, FOX, HBO, BBC, Showtime, Comedy Central, Netflix, Amazon, Hulu, etc., the tone of all these scenes match something that is out there in the marketplace.

Customize Scenes for Yourself

With that in mind, feel free to adapt these to your liking. The heavy lifting is all done. If you need to rearrange some words or edit them down for time, by all means, do. I encourage everyone to read through all the scenes and not take the gender casting too literally. There are lots of opportunities to enhance the unique nature of these original scenes by being creative with the casting. Some of you guys might find comedy gold in the female/female scenes. Ladies, they say it's a man's world. I don't really believe it, but it's fun to speak like them sometimes.

The Heroes & Heroines of Comedy

One of the most valuable components of our curriculum at Actors Comedy Studio is The Heroes & Heroines of Comedy: ten distinct archetypes, used by writers to create specific characters, especially within half-hour comedy. I have included them in this book in an abbreviated form for you to use as breakdowns for your scenes. After the title of the scene, you'll see the character age and their archetype.

While you're more than welcome to play the scene however you like, I know what I was shooting for when I created each character. Hopefully, this extra bit of information will garner you greater success playing each scene. They all come with a breakdown!

The extended value of this book is ultimately the clarity with which you can cast yourself. No one knows you better than you. If you are an actor in the process of building a career and need a scene for agent, manager or casting director meetings, I strongly advise you to cast yourself in the most believable role possible, suited to your strengths or wheelhouse.

If you're a student actor, then the sky's the limit. Maybe you don't even know what your type is yet or how you'll be cast. Play around with different scenes and archetypes and not only will you have a good time, you'll end up discovering your voice as an actor and start understanding what feels most honest to you. Ultimately, that is how casting would place you.

Shoot Reel Footage

Lastly, I know a lot of actors who need reel footage but are reluctant to self-produce largely for fear of writing or lack of experience. I'd like to help solve that problem, too. If you want to shoot and edit these scenes, you're more than welcome to! Each scene is three to six minutes long. You only need 30 seconds or so to create a clip. Here is some insight into how agents and managers submit actors to casting directors and why footage is so important, if you don't already know.

Professional actors don't need "reels" as much as individual clips at this point. Casting doesn't have the need or desire to watch several minutes (or even one minute) of a developing actor's footage. It's not a piece of entertainment to them and they get several thousand submissions for even the smallest roles. It's merely a tool to quickly see what you're like and if you seem experienced enough to bring in for an audition. Some actors still have reels, but future actors won't even use that term. I've already eliminated it from my vocabulary.

How Casting Works in Hollywood

Casting brings in actors who are submitted by agents and managers through Breakdown Services. What they see is an actor's profile on Actors Access. This can be a little confusing, but in a nutshell Breakdown Services and Actors Access are the same entity. Actors create a profile on Actors Access. Agents and mangers submit the link to your profile digitally to casting directors. Casting views those submissions on Breakdown Services. Actors do not have access to Breakdown Services. It's the same company with two different login portals: one for actors and another for casting directors. Think of it as a front door and a back door to the same house, but with different locks. Virtually every show you watch on a screen utilizes this system to cast actors.

Actors Access encourages you to upload multiple digital clips that are individually labeled, as opposed to one long reel. This provides agents and actors the ability to be as specific as possible when choosing a headshot and clip for a submission and is much more efficient for casting directors. For example, attaching a clip that's titled, "Neurotic First Date," is better than attaching a general, one-minute long reel.

So, since these scenes feature characters that have clear definition, and because you can customize the lines, this is a terrific opportunity for emerging (or established) actors to get new footage shot with material you can trust.

The industry needs actors to offer up footage. We're past the point that you can realistically expect to acquire representation and book acting work without it. I'm excited to see what comes from this offer. If you do shoot something I've written, you can send me a link at Gunnar@actorscomedystudio.com and I'll check it out!

How Not to Use This Book

Any use of the material in this book, in any form, for financial gain of any amount is expressly illegal and forbidden.

TABLE OF CONTENTS

TABLE OF CONTENTS

Male & Female Scenes (cont'd)

TABLE OF CONTENTS

TABLE OF CONTENTS

THE HEROES & HEROINES OF COMEDY

Anchor

Smart, Sarcastic, Responsible, Tolerant, Direct

Dependable, stable and straightforward, the Anchor teaches those around them how to live life responsibly. They can be bossy know-it-alls, but they are also caring and nurturing. The Anchor functions as a parent within their tribe, whether they have actual children or not. In turn, they take on unnecessary responsibility and complain about it a lot, which can make them a martyr. With no quirks, they rely heavily on sarcasm to produce humor and vent their frustration in small doses.

Mantra: *"I teach"*
Strength: *Grounded*
Weakness: *Codependent*

Examples:

Michael Bluth (Jason Bateman), *Arrested Development*

Dorothy Zbornak (Bea Arthur), *The Golden Girls*

Dreamer

Hopeful, Persistent, Charismatic, Unpredictable, Unsettled

The Dreamer lives life with their heart on their sleeve. Everyone has ambitions, but the Dreamer is driven by unmatched enthusiasm, passion and desperation to get what they want. Dreamers are self-deprecating. They poke fun at themselves before anyone else gets the chance. Dreamers tend to be irresponsible, spontaneous and impulsive. If there's a poorly thought-out plan within the story, the Dreamer is very likely the one executing it. The Dreamer could definitely use a boost of self-esteem.

Mantra: *"I hope"*
Strength: *Resilient*
Weakness: *Immature*

Examples:

Cameron Tucker (Eric Stonestreet), *Modern Family*

Penny (Kaley Cuoco), *The Big Bang Theory*

Neurotic

Anxious, Cerebral, Inflexible, Defensive, Capable

You can feel a Neurotic's energy. It's palpable and sometimes overwhelming. Neurotics are fueled by anxiety and are often high-strung individuals. They are smart and well-educated, usually with a degree-oriented or managerial position in the workplace. They thrive when their environment has order and structure but become prickly and difficult when life becomes chaotic. Neurotics tend to be high achievers in life, but their perfectionism can lead to inflexibility and obsessive-compulsive behaviors.

Mantra: *"I worry"*
Strength: *Organized*
Weakness: *Insecure*

Examples:

Ross Geller (David Schwimmer), *Friends*

Claire Dunphy (Julie Bowen), *Modern Family*

Narcissist

Conceited, Flamboyant, Spoiled, Conservative, Shallow

Self-love is a good thing until it's taken too far. This is the realm of the Narcissist. Shallow, status-conscious and self-possessed, Narcissists like themselves and nice things in exactly that order. They have a flair for theatrics and a sense of entitlement. The Narcissist is in a constant state of awareness and judgment of those around them. They pity those who have less and they're jealous of those who have more. They need a lot of attention. Fortunately, they're flamboyant enough to get it.

Mantra: *"I deserve"*
Strength: *Magnetic*
Weakness: *Intolerant*

Examples:

Schmidt (Max Greenfield), *New Girl*

Mindy Lahiri (Mindy Kaling), *The Mindy Project*

Rebel

Mysterious, Unyielding, Intimidating, Bold, God Complex

It takes a strong, commanding person to change the world and the Rebel is happy to step up to that challenge. Rebels are stoic and edgy with a God Complex. They are often scornful of the way things are done by the minions around them, or of society itself. They have little regard for rules and lead compartmentalized, secretive lives. Adrenaline junkies at heart, the Rebel will always run toward danger when others would run away. The Rebel does not care what others think of them.

Mantra: *"I challenge"*
Strength: *Authoritative*
Weakness: *Lonely*

Examples:

Ron Swanson (Nick Offerman), *Parks and Recreation*

Jackie Peyton (Edie Falco), *Nurse Jackie*

Buffoon

Dimwitted, Competitive, Self-Important, Egotistical, Defiant

The primary component of the Buffoon is that they are socially inept. They are an interesting mix of goofy, antagonistic and dense. They think they're clever, but really, they're full of bluster. The real clown of the bunch, the Buffoon has an unjust amount of confidence that seems to come from nowhere. They often write checks their butts can't cash. You'd feel badly for how often they fall flat on their faces, if it wasn't their own fault. The Buffoon is unnecessarily competitive with those to whom they're the closest, like co-workers, spouses and even their own kids.

Mantra: *"I know"*
Strength: *Passionate*
Weakness: *Delusional*

Examples:

Sheldon Cooper (Jim Parsons), *The Big Bang Theory*

Dawn Forchette (Alex Borstein), *Getting On*

Eccentric

Unconventional, Fierce, Opinionated, Shameless, Unique

By definition, the Eccentric is rare because they see the world through their own prism. They have an overactive imagination and are shameless in expressing their singular point of view about the world as they see it. They are non-judgmental, open and accepting of everyone around them. At first glance, Eccentrics can just seem plain odd, but really, they are fierce and friendly people who are hyper-connected to the world and curious about everything.

Mantra: *"I imagine"*
Strength: *Open*
Weakness: *Misunderstood*

Examples:

Jack McFarland (Sean Hayes), *Will & Grace*

Phoebe Buffay (Lisa Kudrow), *Friends*

Innocent

Joyful, Happy, Honest, Sincere, Childlike

The Innocent is made of love and wants everyone around them to be happy. It's not that they're people pleasers, they simply exude joy with childlike enthusiasm most of the time. Earnest and honest, the Innocent does not use sarcasm and they are the only one of the Heroes and Heroines who does not. They have no edge and no agenda. Their trusting nature is mostly an asset, but they can also be predictably naïve. The upside is, if you need a dose of positivity, the Innocent is always there to provide it.

Mantra: *"I love"*
Strength: *Authentic*
Weakness: *Gullible*

Examples:

Andy Dwyer (Chris Pratt), *Parks and Recreation*

Sue Heck (Eden Sher), *The Middle*

Cynic

Condescending, Dry, Bitter, Wise, Street Smart

Always waiting for the other shoe to drop, the Cynic sees the glass half-empty. Generally pessimistic, they are the perennial voice of doubt. Although they can be snide and short-tempered, Cynics come packed with wisdom and street smarts. They are also good friends to have because they understand how the real world works and will always shoot straight with you. Once you've won over a Cynic, they will have your back forever. They're equal parts jaded and dutifully reliable.

Mantra: *"I doubt"*
Strength: *Loyal*
Weakness: *Guarded*

Examples:

Frank Barone (Peter Boyle), *Everybody Loves Raymond*

Sue Wilson (Sufe Bradshaw), *Veep*

Player

Seductive, Sensual, Vain, Aggressive, Smooth

Someone has to make everyday life sexy and that's where the Player comes in. We all have sexual impulses, but the Player has more of them, more of the time. Constantly on the prowl, the Player lives for sexual conquest. Seductive and smooth, they see the world through a filter of lust. Forward and flirtatious, the Player is brave and unflinching about getting whatever they desire. They can be a bit too single-minded in their quest for pleasure, but they're always fun to have around.

Mantra: *"I lust"*
Strength: *Confident*
Weakness: *Noncommittal*

Examples:

Barney Stinson (Neil Patrick Harris), *How I Met Your Mother*

Samantha Jones (Kim Cattrall), *Sex and the City*

MALE & FEMALE SCENES

BEDHEAD

INT. BEDROOM - EVENING

NIKKI AND ED ARE CURLED UP IN BED NEXT
TO EACH OTHER. THEY CLEARLY JUST HAD A
"SPECIAL TIME" TOGETHER.

> NIKKI
> That was great.

> ED
> Unbelievable.

> NIKKI
> You're unbelievable.

> ED
> No, you are.

> NIKKI
> You are.

> ED
> No, you are.

> NIKKI
> Stop it. You're silly.

> ED
> I'm just happy. You make me happy.

> NIKKI
> Oh... Ed.

NIKKI SWOONS. ED CLOSES HIS EYES TO SLEEP.
BEAT.

ED
Can you let go now?

NIKKI
Hmmm?

ED
Can you please let go of me?

NIKKI
But... I was just cuddling.

ED
I know. I'm done. Thanks.

NIKKI TAKES A BEAT TO RECOVER.

NIKKI
Um, Ed?

ED
Yeah?

NIKKI
That was rude.

ED
Oh. I'm sorry. Thanks very much for
the great sex and awesome cuddling. I
just don't like to be touched aside
from sex. G'night.

ED GIVES NIKKI A PECK ON THE CHEEK AND GOES
BACK TO SLEEP.

                    NIKKI
Ed!

                    ED
Yuh-huh?

                    NIKKI
What do you mean aside from sex? You
mean right after sex, right?

                    ED
No. I mean, I don't like to be touched
aside from sex. Was I unclear?

                    NIKKI
So if I touched you right now, you'd
have a problem with it?

                    ED
Unless it was more sexy touch, yes.

                    NIKKI
That's... well, I think I have a
problem with that.

                    ED
Are you judging me?

                    NIKKI
Yes, I think I am!

                    ED
Well, now who's being rude?!

NIKKI

Well, I'm sorry. I don't think I can
sleep in a bed all night with someone
who doesn't like to even be touched.

ED

Aside from sex! (THEN) I asked you
nicely. Why is this such a big deal?

NIKKI

Because I'm a woman and I just gave
myself to you in a private and very
uninhibited way. I don't want to hear,
"don't touch me" after what I just did
to your hoo-ha!

ED

And I don't want you to touch me aside
from touching my hoo-ha! People don't
touch each other more than they do!
Correct?!

NIKKI

Of course that's correct, Nimrod!
That's not the point. You're not
hearing me!

ED

Okay. Let's do this over. Nikki, I
love making love to women. In fact,
I think I'm really good at it. But
that's the only time I like to be
touched. Otherwise, it gives me the
willies. It's just the way I am. I've
always been that way and I can't help
it. Are we good?

                    NIKKI
No, I feel violated.

                    ED
Not more so than I.

                    NIKKI
You need to look into this, my friend!
I'm serious. You can't seduce a woman,
take her to bed, be inside of her
then tell her she can't touch you.
Women aren't wired that way. We need
affection, connection, intimacy...

                    ED
Flowers, notes, eye contact!

                    NIKKI
What?!

                    ED
I bring flowers to every important
occasion; affection. I leave nice
notes, sometimes poems, on the night
stand; connection. I can sustain eye
contact with my partner indefinitely;
intimacy!

HE LOCKS EYES WITH HER. IT'S INTENSE. MAYBE
THIS IS TURNING AROUND, THEN...

                    NIKKI
But you can't hold my hand?

                    ED
Jesus, would you let it go?

                    NIKKI
No, I can't. I feel like that's all
a very elaborate way to keep yourself
isolated within a relationship. It's
selfish and I'm calling bullshit on
it. What would our children think if
they never saw us touch each other?

                    ED
I met you last week.

                    NIKKI
Hypothetically. I'm not in love with
you. But someday you're going to have
to work this out with some woman at
some point because it's so totally
fucking obnoxious. I just happen to be
nice enough to try and help.

                    ED
Nikki... I do not think you're nice.

                    NIKKI
Fine. Maybe I'm not. But at least I'm
open to feedback.

                    ED
I think I should go.

                    NIKKI
Agreed. I'll hold still while you
leave the bed. I wouldn't want my calf
to brush against your foot.

ED DRESSES HIMSELF.

                    ED
We all have issues, okay? At least
some of us are brave enough to express
them and trusting enough to hope
others will accept them.

                    NIKKI
Yes, well the issue scale was tipping
a little too far on your side, so...

                    ED
Good luck with your intolerance.

                    NIKKI
Yeah, right. Good luck with your
avoidant personality disorder.

EARFUCK

<u>INT. OFFICE - DAY</u>

VICKI BACKS IN THROUGH THE DOOR AS KYLE IS
BUSY WORKING AT HIS DESK. THERE IS ANOTHER
EMPTY DESK BESIDE HIS. SHE IS FINISHING OFF
A CONVERSATION WITH SOMEONE IN THE HALL.

                VICKI
Thanks for the directions, I never
would've found it without you! Why
don't you stop by sometime and we'll
have a coffee break together. Yeah,
just whenever. Okay, see ya', bye! (TO
HERSELF) What a nice janitor!

SHE TURNS INTO THE ROOM AND SEES KYLE.

              VICKI (CONT'D)
Oh, hi! You must be Kyle, my new
office mate! Or, well, I'm Vicki, your
new office mate. I guess that would
be a better way of putting it, since
you already work here and I'm new.
(SHE SNORT LAUGHS) Oh, excuse me, I'm
being so rude. That wasn't really a
proper introduction. My whole name
is Victoria Maria Sparello, but my
friends call me Vicki and I understand
from the memo I received from Human
Resources (SHE AWKWARDLY DIGS IT OUT
OF THE BOX SHE'S CARRYING) that I
am to share an office with one...
(REFERRING TO MEMO) Kyle Haggerty and
I certainly hope that's you or I'm
gonna have to do this whole darn thing
over with someone else and that would

                    VICKI (CONT'D)
be the dang-diddliest thing that's
happened to me today!

                    KYLE
Ah...

                    VICKI
Oh my gosh, this isn't a surprise,
is it? That I'm going to be your new
office mate? Because if you didn't
even know this would be embarrassing
on top of awkward on top of - Oh, I
don't even know what else it would be,
but I'll tell ya' what, I've found
from experience that if I'm searching
for an idea or I've lost my train of
thought or anything like that, I can
just keep talking my way into finding
the idea or remembering what I've
forgotten, if that happened to be the
case, so if I come to the end of a
sentence and I don't have the - Oh,
wait! Mortifying! That's what else
it could be! Embarrassing, awkward
and mortifying. And I certainly
hope it isn't any of those things
because if you are Kyle, we'll be
working together for a long, long,
longlonglong time. Are you Kyle?

THERE IS A LONG BEAT AS KYLE TRIES TO
DECIDE IF HE'LL BE ABLE TO SPEAK.

KYLE
Yes. Welcome to Taxmasters.

SHE SMILES. HE GESTURES TO THE OTHER
DESK.

VICKI	KYLE (CONT'D)
Why don't I just put my things over here on this empty desk, since there are obviously only two desks and you're using that one, so it would only make perfect sense that I use this one, which is great because if I sit here, I'll be facing north, which is a good direction for me, because when I think of "north," I think of "up," which makes me think of moving up in my career, or just keeping my attitude up, which is important, I think, for everyone, but especially me, because I am prone to bouts of serious seasonal depression	Why don't you just-

VICKI (CONT'D)
and that's no fun
for me or anyone else
around me, so who's
a lucky duck today?
Northward facing
Vicki, that's who!
Boy, Kyle, you sure
are quiet. Cat got
your tongue?

KYLE
I'm just... wow, I'm working. I'm
trying to work. We've had a lot of
tax returns come in late this year, so
I'm working on them. And now I have a
headache.

VICKI	KYLE (CONT'D)
Oh, boy, do I	No, that's okay...
have just the	forget I said
thing for that	anything. Just drop
- I don't know	it, Vicki... VICKI!
if you believe	Please! Can you just
in traditional	STOP talking?
medicine	
or Eastern	
medicine or if	
you belong to	
some Orthodox	
religion where	
you can't take-	

VICKI
Yes, I can. (THEN) I'm so sorry, Kyle.

> VICKI (CONT'D)
> I completely apologize. I just burst
> in here without any thought of your
> needs and I will stop talking, but I
> just have to make it up to you first,
> just tell me what I can do -

> KYLE
> I did. I did tell you what to do! I
> told you to stop talking and then you
> didn't do that. What's wrong with you?

> VICKI
> I don't know. Do I talk a lot? No
> one's ever pointed that out before.

> KYLE
> Because they never had a chance!

> VICKI   KYLE (CONT'D)
> Oh my God,   Quit it... quit it...
> something is   quit it, Vicki, QUIT
> wrong with me   IT!
> and I never
> knew it!
> Maybe I have
> some kind of
> disorder or
> disability...

> KYLE (CONT'D)
> My God! It's like you're stabbing my
> ears with your mouth.

                    VICKI
(COMPLETELY OFFENDED/OUTRAGED)
Really??!! I have never been spoken to
that way in my life! (THEN SHE REVERTS
COMPLETELY BACK TO BUBBLY VICKI) Well,
there was that one time in Brisbane -

                    KYLE
Stop it, or I will kill you. I will
pick up this laptop and shove it into
your mouth then go into the supply
closet, get twelve rolls of duct tape
and wrap it around your flappity,
jabbery jaw and I will kill you, you
ear fucker!

                    VICKI
That was a very mean thing to say.

                    KYLE
It was. I was... trying to tell you
how I was feeling, and it came out
more... murderous than I intended. I
apologize -

VICKI TRIES TO ACCEPT.

                    KYLE (CONT'D)
BUT, I don't want you to respond to
it.

VICKI PUTS HER HAND OVER HER MOUTH, CLEARLY
STRUGGLING NOT TO SPEAK.

                    KYLE (CONT'D)
I don't think this is going to work.

VICKI TRIES TO AGREE.

> KYLE (CONT'D)
> Shhh! I was only doing this for extra
> cash, but I don't think I want the
> money that badly anymore. In fact, I'm
> sure of it. I would rather maintain
> high levels of credit card debt with
> bad interest rates. So have the office
> and have a nice life, Vicki.

> VICKI
> Goodb-

> KYLE
> Don't!

KYLE EXITS.

> VICKI
> Boy, Vicki, you sure didn't make a
> good first impression. Maybe you are
> a chatterbox. Maybe? Of course you
> are. You're a talker, girl. You talk
> in your sleep. You talk to yourself.
> You're talking to yourself right now.

VICKI GETS BACK TO UNPACKING HER BOX, BUT
NEVER STOPS TALKING.

> VICKI (CONT'D)
> Yeah, but they say people who talk to
> themselves are generally happier than
> people who don't and it doesn't mean

                    VICKI (CONT'D)
        you're crazy, it just means you're
        comfortable with your own thoughts...

LIGHTS FADE.

EGGED

INT. BRIAN'S OFFICE - AFTERNOON

BRIAN IS BUSY WORKING AS HIS EX-WIFE,
DIANE, ENTERS AND SITS.

            DIANE
 I just met your new secretary. She
looks cheap.

            BRIAN
Hello, Diane. Good to see you're
well and spreading joy throughout the
land. What's so urgent that you had
to barge into my office on a Wednesday
afternoon?

            DIANE
We have business to discuss.

            BRIAN
Ah! That's the wonder of being
divorced, kid. We have no business
to discuss. Unless one of the kids
is dead or in jail. Is one of our
beautiful children dead or in jail?

            DIANE
Thanks to me, no.

            BRIAN
Then we have no business.

            DIANE
It pains me to say, but we have
unfinished business, Brian.

> BRIAN

Diane, we spent the better part of
a year hammering out the details
of our divorce. As I remember it,
I was generous, you were awful and
our lawyers got a whole bunch of our
money. What did we possibly miss?

> DIANE

My eggs. And I was accommodating as
hell, you cheating rat bastard. We
missed my eggs.

> BRIAN

I'm sorry. Have you finally flipped?
Are we reopening our settlement over
the contents of our refrigerator?

> DIANE

Don't be a jackass, Brian. MY EGGS!

> BRIAN

Your... Oh. The frozen ones. I forgot.

> DIANE

I did too. For Christ's sake, it was
twenty years ago.

> BRIAN

Are they still good?

> DIANE

Apparently. I mean, it's not
guaranteed, but, probably. We went to
the best fertility clinic in the

DIANE (CONT'D)
country. Anyway, I was shredding some
paperwork and our wedding album -
things that reminded me of you - and I
found the registration forms for the
cryopreservation.

BRIAN
Which turned out to be completely
unnecessary because we got drunk and
celebrated after the procedure and...

DIANE
I got pregnant with Jessica.

BRIAN
And you said -

DIANE
Let's keep them just in case.

BRIAN
And then right after Jessica -

DIANE
I said, "Let's have another one right
away because it will be easier to
raise two at the same age -

BRIAN
-and we can have another one later."

DIANE
Which we never got around to and the

                    DIANE (CONT'D)
eggs just stayed in the bank. Well,
it's time to make a withdrawal, Brian.
But I can't do it without you.

                    BRIAN
Why's that?

                    DIANE
You wrote the check. They're MY eggs,
but you paid the clinic. They're the
last things that belong to both of us.
I need you to spring my girls.

                    BRIAN
Fine. What do I need to do?

                    DIANE
Just sign this and I'll take care of
the rest.

BRIAN TAKES THE DOCUMENT AND SIGNS IT.

                    BRIAN
What do you mean the rest?

                    DIANE
I mean... I'm thinking about having
another baby.

                    BRIAN
You're sixty!

                    DIANE
I know how old I am, Brian. I'm

DIANE (CONT'D)
looking for a suitable surrogate.
Once I find one, I'll go to a sperm
bank, get my eggs out of the egg bank,
fertilize them and make a baby with a
nice young girl who needs twenty-five
thousand dollars and then leaves my
life forever.

BRIAN
Are you drunk?

DIANE
Don't belittle my ambitions, Brian.
That's just like you! Every time I've
figured out what I want out of this
life, you try to make me question it.
Well, those days are over, pal. I feel
like being a mom again and that's all
the reason I need to do it.

BRIAN
Diane, I am not making fun of your...
scheme. I'm genuinely concerned. Have
you really thought this through? We
are not young people.

DIANE
Our kids don't want kids, Brian.

BRIAN
God, they're smart.

DIANE
I should be a grandma by now. It's not
going to happen. I miss being around

                DIANE (CONT'D)
a new life. As I was destroying the
remnants of ours, I realized I had one
last chance.

                BRIAN
Then... good luck.

                DIANE
Thank you.

                BRIAN
You know, if you want to skip the sperm
bank, I'd be more than happy to -

                DIANE
Oh, God no. That actually just made
me a little nauseous. I'll let myself
out. Say hi to your trophy wife.

DIANE EXITS.

                BRIAN
Her name is Brittany! (SOTTO) Ah, she
knows what her name is.

EXISTENTIALIST

INT. LIVING ROOM - AFTERNOON

DEB IS READING A MAGAZINE. MARTIN IS
WORKING ON A THESIS.

> MARTIN
> Do you ever wonder why we're here?
> What all this really means?

> DEB
> Yes. Everybody does. Stop talking
> about it.

> MARTIN
> Deb! This is important. I'm pondering
> the meaning of life.

> DEB
> Uh-huh. I know. Stop.

> MARTIN
> But I need to get this paper written
> for my philosophy class and it's
> really got me thinking about what
> we're all doing here.

> DEB
> I'll tell you. I'm reading. You're
> engaging in futility.

> MARTIN
> Futile? How is learning futile?

> DEB
> What you're wondering about is

DEB (CONT'D)
unlearnable, so quit it.

MARTIN
Oh, my God. You are not an
intellectually curious person.

DEB
What? That's not true.

MARTIN
It is. That's why you don't read food
labels or use your iPhone for anything
but making phone calls.

DEB
Shut up, I use apps. Why are you
torturing me?

MARTIN
I'm worried about your spiritual
outlook. I think you're not thinking
about the bigger picture.

DEB
Just because I don't want to talk to
you about it doesn't mean I haven't
thought about it. Life is supposed to
be mysterious. Buy into it.

MARTIN
I disagree! I think we're supposed to
learn and evolve and reach for answers
even if we never get them.

                    DEB
Which is futile!

                  MARTIN
How do you know if you don't try?

                    DEB
I did! And I didn't get the desired
results. Do you know what "futile"
means?

                  MARTIN
Listen. We have been best friends
since college. You were a downer
then and, frankly, nothing much has
changed. But I'll be darned if I sit
idly by while you turn into a hopeless
curmudgeon without any zest for the
rest of the life we have left to live!

                    DEB
Jesus, who pushed your "go" button? My
life is exactly how I like it, thank
you very much! I have a fulfilling
friends-with-benefits situation
happening with Frank Rodgers on my
bowling league, so I get lots of
better than average, blue collar sex.
I'm a hospice care nurse, so I'll
never not have a job and I don't waste
any time worrying about where I was
before this or where I'm heading after
because we were obviously not meant to
know!

                    MARTIN
OR that could easily be interpreted
as a challenge to never stop trying
to figure it out! What if the sheer
questioning of it all is the highest
state of being?

                    DEB
Holy fuck, I'm having an epiphany!

                    MARTIN
Yeah?!

                    DEB
Yeah, you know that saying, about the
definition of insanity... doing the
same thing over and over again and
getting the same result?

                    MARTIN
Yeah?

                    DEB
They were thinking of you!

                    MARTIN
Well, excuse me for envisioning you as
a celestial being, who has a spirit
and a soul and isn't just a bag of
flesh with a bunch of bones inside.

                    DEB
Not a problem. Is this discussion
over?

> MARTIN
I'm tenacious, Deb. I don't give up on
things just because they're difficult.
Apparently, that makes one of us.

MARTIN GOES BACK TO WRITING. DEB RETURNS TO
HER MAGAZINE.

> MARTIN (CONT'D)
Ass.

> DEB
Are you mad at me because I don't want
to talk to you about the meaning of
life?

> MARTIN
Yes.

> DEB
Are you serious?

> MARTIN
Yes.

> DEB
Will you let me finish this magazine
if I tell you?

> MARTIN
Yes.

> DEB
I think life is meaningful only
as long as we learn from each new
experience and nothing more than that

DEB (CONT'D)
is expected of us.

MARTIN
Wow. That's so simple and eloquent,
Deb. I love that.

DEB
But I could be wrong, so why bother
talking about it?

MARTIN
You are a despicable human being!

DEB
Really? What does that mean?

FUDGED

INT. LIVING ROOM - AFTERNOON

NICOLE IS ON HER PHONE, WATCHING TV.

                    NICOLE
        Well, personally, I could never be
        with a man who likes *Rock of Ages*
        more than *Hamilton*. I mean, what a
        dipshit...

THERE IS A KNOCK ON THE DOOR. NICOLE
AD-LIBS A GOODBYE AND ANSWERS.

                    NICOLE (CONT'D)
        Dad!

NICOLE'S FATHER, HAROLD, APPEARS IN THE
DOORWAY AND BARGES RIGHT IN.

                    HAROLD
        I should've called first, I know, but
        I need to talk to you about something.

                    NICOLE
        Is everything alright?

                    HAROLD
        No, actually. (DEEP BREATH) Oh boy,
        how am I going to say this? I have a
        confession to make.

                    NICOLE
        Okay, sit down.

                    HAROLD
        You see, I was at this AA meeting and

HAROLD (CONT'D)
part of the whole program is to make
amends -

NICOLE
Oh, thank God. We were all kind've
worried. What made you realize you
needed help?

HAROLD
I'm not an alcoholic, I'm just dating
one.

NICOLE
Oh. Oh! (THEN, BRIGHTLY) You met
someone? That is so great! I mean if
she stays on the wagon. Is she pretty?

HAROLD
Just listen! I was sitting at the
meeting listening to everyone talk
about how they... wronged people in
their lives and feeling guilty, and
well...

NICOLE
Are you making amends with me?

HAROLD
Here's the deal, sweetie. When you
were born, your mom and I weren't
married yet. People were less liberal
about these things back then, so to
spare you and us any embarrassment we,
uh, well... fudged your age a little
to match when we actually got married.

                    NICOLE
    What do you mean, "fudged"?

                    HAROLD
    Changed. Amended. Distorted... perhaps
    grossly.

                    NICOLE
    So, I'm not turning twenty-nine next
    week?

HAROLD SHAKES HIS HEAD "NO".

                    NICOLE (CONT'D)
    I'm going to be thirty?

HAROLD GESTURES WITH HIS THUMB - HIGHER.

                    NICOLE (CONT'D)
    ...thirty-one?

                    HAROLD
    Four.

                    NICOLE
    Shut your mouth! I'm thirty-four?
    My horoscope said to expect bad news
    today, but I didn't expect this...
    fuck.

                    HAROLD
    Well, you probably read the wrong one.
    You're actually not a Cancer.

                    NICOLE
Dad! This is insane. Why did it take
you and mom so long to get married?

                    HAROLD
Drugs.

                    NICOLE
AND?!

                    HAROLD
Oh, that's the whole answer. Just
drugs. But you were always safe. We
lived in a commune at the time. I
think your immune system's so good
because you were breastfed by so many
different women.

                    NICOLE
You've never been responsible. I don't
know why I'm surprised! People need
to ease into their thirties, Dad. Not
be thrown straight into the middle of
them!

                    HAROLD
Imagine if I'd waited longer. You're
welcome!

                    NICOLE
Oh, shit... I can't breathe. I'm so
goddamn old. I think I'm going to
hyperventilate.

HAROLD
Do you need a Heimlich?

NICOLE
I'M NOT CHOKING! I need a drink. And a
time machine! You know, at this point
you could have just never told me and
let me be happy. Did you think of that?!

HAROLD
No. I have bad boundaries and non-
existent social skills. That's why
your mom left me. Are you mad?

NICOLE
I'm fucking furious! I was going to
bungee jump on my thirtieth. Now I'm
supposed to have already done that and
have way more money in my IRA. It's
going to take me a while to process
this.

HAROLD
We'll discuss it more, I promise,
but I need to break the news to your
sister. If I don't do it now, I might
lose my nerve.

NICOLE
What do you have to tell Leslie?

HAROLD
Your mom and I were married when we
had her, but we didn't want a big gap
in your ages, so we lied the other way
with her. She's thirty. So you're not

               HAROLD (CONT'D)
the baby anymore, either. She is. They
say that stuff matters, but ahhhh.
You're okay, right?

               NICOLE
Okay? Why on earth would -

               HAROLD
That's my strong girl. I knew you'd be
a trooper.

HAROLD KISSES HER ON THE FOREHEAD AND EXITS
IN A HURRY. NICOLE LOOKS AT A STRAY HAIR.

               NICOLE
Oh, fan-fucking-tastic! It's grey!

HEAVEN

INT. BAR - LATE AFTERNOON

HEAVEN, A PROSTITUTE, SITS AT A BAR. SHE IS
DISENCHANTED AND UNINTERESTED IN WHAT IS
GOING ON AROUND HER. SHE PROBABLY SPENDS A
LOT OF TIME HERE.

SHE HAS A MOMENT ALONE, DRINKING AND
SMOKING UNTIL CHARLIE ENTERS AND SITS NEXT
TO HER. INITIALLY, SHE DOES NOT RESPOND.

                    CHARLIE
          Hello. My name is Charlie Mascardo.
          I've never been to the Frolic Room
          before. This is my first time.

HEAVEN NODS DISDAINFULLY, THEN LOOKS AWAY.

                    CHARLIE
          Well, you're no Chatty Cathy, are you?

HEAVEN SIMULTANEOUSLY TAKES A DRINK AND
SHAKES HER HEAD "NO".

                    CHARLIE (CONT'D)
          What's your name?

                    HEAVEN
          Heaven.

                    CHARLIE
          Well, that's very interesting. What's
          your last name?

                    HEAVEN
          Earth.

                    CHARLIE
        (MINI-BEAT) Oh, I see. I guess that
        would make your middle name...

            HEAVEN   CHARLIE (CONT'D)
            "On".   "On".

                 CHARLIE (CONT'D)
        Yes, it would. You're a prostitute,
        aren't you?

                     HEAVEN
        (SIGHS) Yes. And no offense to you,
        Charlie, but I charge for my time.

PULLS A TWENTY OUT OF HIS WALLET.

                    CHARLIE
        Well then, you up for some
        conversation?

                     HEAVEN
        (SHE TAKES THE MONEY) It's your dime,
        start talkin'.

                    CHARLIE
        First, I'd love a Tic Tac. Do you have
        any?

                     HEAVEN
        (FINDING IT AN ODD REQUEST) Yeah. (SHE
        GETS THEM OUT OF HER PURSE)

                    CHARLIE
        Oh good, I knew you would. I had a
        friend who was a prostitute once

CHARLIE (CONT'D)
and she always had Tic Tacs in her
purse. Tic Tacs and a New York Times
crossword puzzle. She's dead now.

HEAVEN
That's too bad. How'd she die?

CHARLIE
I don't know, I didn't ask. I find
death disturbing.

HEAVEN
(UNFAZED) I find life disturbing.

CHARLIE
EEWWW! You just revealed something
about yourself. Did you mean to?

HEAVEN
So what if I did? We're having
a conversation, right? You have
a conversation, you talk about
yourself... geesh!

CHARLIE
Oh yes, of course. You're absolutely
right. Maybe I should reveal something
about myself then. Okay, here goes...
I spent all of last year quietly
falling apart in a rented room above a
bakery in West Hollywood.

HEAVEN
(GIVES HIM THE ONCE OVER) Surprise,
surprise.

CHARLIE
I feel much better now though. You can only cry into a sourdough baguette for so long.

HEAVEN
What's wrong with you?

CHARLIE
Let's just say... my life got to be a little too much.

HEAVEN
My life never amounts to enough.

CHARLIE
(EXCITEDLY) OOHHHH! I love when you do that! Tell me something else about yourself.

HEAVEN
Okay. I get lonely sometimes.

CHARLIE
Maybe that's because you're a whore!

HEAVEN
What?! Fuck you!

CHARLIE
Oh, no, no, no. I don't mean it in a bad way. I just mean that if all you ever have is loveless sex, you're bound to end up feeling, well... solitary.

                    HEAVEN
Fine then, but you watch your step!
Twenty bucks only gets you so far.

                    CHARLIE
I'm just empathizing, Heaven. I've
been through the desert on a horse
with no name myself. You're feisty,
aren't you?

                    HEAVEN
(LAUGHS SOFTLY) You are one weird
dude, Charlie Mascardo.

                    CHARLIE
Well, I get lonely too sometimes,
Heaven On Earth.

                    HEAVEN
I guess we have something in common,
then.

                    CHARLIE
No, not really. You're a whore!

                    HEAVEN
HEY!

                    CHARLIE
Just kidding. Only kidding.

HEAVEN LAUGHS AND SHAKES HER HEAD.

                    CHARLIE (CONT'D)
You're a nice girl, Heaven. You

CHARLIE (CONT'D)
deserve a good man who would treat you
well.

HEAVEN
I know I do, Charlie. And I think he
might even be out there waiting for
me. But I'll be damned if I've found
him yet.

CHARLIE
I'm a good man, Heaven.

HEAVEN
I know you are, Charlie. You're also
too goddamn weird to be believed.

CHARLIE
Oh, well, really. Don't hold back now.

HEAVEN
(WITH A WINK) Just kidding.

CHARLIE
Oh, yes. Of course you are.

HEAVEN
So what do you do for a living,
Charlie?

CHARLIE
I build miniature grandfather clocks.
Here, you can have this one.

HE PULLS A MINIATURE GRANDFATHER CLOCK OUT
OF HIS JACKET POCKET.

HEAVEN
Thanks. Does it work?

CHARLIE
No.

HEAVEN
Oh. Well, thanks anyway.

CHARLIE
Don't mention it. There's plenty more where that came from. Sales have been slow for a while.

HEAVEN
Yeah, times are tough. The economy's in a real slump these days.

CHARLIE
Is it? I guess perhaps that's the problem, then.

HEAVEN
(GIVES A BEWILDERED LOOK) Charlie... do you even know what year it is?

CHARLIE
Really, Heaven! I may be out of touch, but there's certainly no need to talk to me as if I'm insane!

HEAVEN
(BEAT) Who's the president then?

                    CHARLIE
Beats me.

                    HEAVEN
Don't worry, Charlie. That'll be our
little secret.

                    CHARLIE
Mmmm. Imagine that. A tight-lipped
prostitute. Well, I think it's time I
run home now. It's almost midnight. I
want to make sure I can still catch an
Uber.

                    HEAVEN
You can always get an Uber, Charlie.

                    CHARLIE
Not without an app! I hail them
like cabs. They don't like it, but
eventually someone takes pity.

                    HEAVEN
How... brave?

                    CHARLIE
And then it's off to bed. But before
I go to sleep, I think I will open my
diary and write, "Dear Diary, tonight
for twenty dollars I had a little bit
of Heaven On Earth." Poetic, isn't it?

                    HEAVEN
Nice try, Charlie. I saw it coming a
mile away.

                    CHARLIE
(PLACES HIS HAND ON HER ARM) Can't
blame a guy for trying, can you?

                    HEAVEN
(LOOKS DOWN AT HIS HAND AND THEN BACK
UP AT HIM) That costs extra, Charlie.

                    CHARLIE
I'm leaving. (TURNS TO GO) But I might
come back tomorrow night. If I do, it
would be around the same time. And of
course, I'd probably sit in the same
place.

                    HEAVEN
I'll be here, Charlie.

                    CHARLIE
Oh, goody.

INKED

INT. APARTMENT - EVENING

JACKIE AND HECTOR ENTER HIS APARTMENT
SMILING AND CHATTY. THEY'RE ON A DATE
THAT'S GOING GREAT.

                    JACKIE
          That was amazing. I have literally
          never seen a movie outside before.

                    HECTOR
          Seriously?

                    JACKIE
          Watching *Beetlejuice* in a park
          and eating from a food truck is
          ridonkulous. I would literally do it a
          million more times.

                    HECTOR
          Wow. I am so relieved. I'm not going
          to lie, Jackie. I have been sweating
          this date since we met on Tinder.
          Girls like you don't usually respond
          to guys like me.

                    JACKIE
          What do you mean, Hector?

                    HECTOR
          Oh, come on. Don't make me say it. You
          know.

                    JACKIE
          No. No, I really don't.

                    HECTOR
Ah, geez. (THEN) You're a beautiful
girl, Jackie. You're all put together
and shit. I'm from the hood. I work at
a dispensary and do really dark slam
poetry because I can't afford therapy.

                    JACKIE
Right, you're a poet. Like Walt
Whitman.

                    HECTOR
I'm tatted, Jackie. I'm a homie.
I'm not like Walt Whitman. More like
Walter White.

THERE'S A SUDDEN TURN. JACKIE, LET'S SAY...
IGNITES SEXUALLY.

                    JACKIE
Oh, the tattoos. Yes, you have lots of
tattoos. You have ink all over, don't
you? Your skeleton's like an easel for
the canvas of your skin. You're just
missing the frame. Where do they stop,
Hector?

                    HECTOR
Huh?

                    JACKIE
What haven't I seen yet?

HECTOR IS TAKEN ABACK.

> HECTOR
> I don't know... whatever's under my
> shirt and pants.

> JACKIE
> I want to see your secret meat marks,
> Hector. Yes, I inky-dinky do.

> HECTOR
> They're not secret, I just have
> clothes on.

> JACKIE
> Well, let's fix that!

SHE POUNCES ON HIM. HE WARDS HER OFF.

> HECTOR
> What the fuck just happened to you?
> Are you half panther? Jesus, you're
> like a werepanther.

> JACKIE
> You are literally everything I have
> dreamt of since I was thirteen,
> Hector, and I will literally do
> anything my body is physically capable
> of doing to bring you pleasure. I am a
> gymnast and a yoga instructor.

> HECTOR
> Whoa! Slow way the hell down. What do you
> mean 'everything you've dreamt of?' We
> just met tonight and ate Koji Barbecue on
> a blanket. You don't know me.

                    JACKIE
Don't I?

                    HECTOR
Fuck no.

                    JACKIE
You're intelligent. Sensitive. You're
artistic, kind and determined to make
the rest of your life better than the
first part. Correct?

                    HECTOR
Well -

                    JACKIE
But you look like you should be in
prison.

                    HECTOR
Hey!

                    JACKIE
IS THAT ALSO CORRECT?!

                    HECTOR
Yes! I mean, no - it's... super
fuckin' stereotypical, but I guess.
What is your point?

                    JACKIE
You're a good guy, Hector Ignacio
Salazar. A good guy who looks like
a bad boy. You'll treat me like a
princess and piss off my father the

                    JACKIE (CONT'D)
second he sees you. God, I want to
piss him off! We both know I'm better
than you, so you'll be loyal like a
dog and I won't have to worry about
you cheating. You pulled yourself
out of a gang, so you know what real
danger is and my guess is that's got
to show up between the sheets. You
check every one of my boxes, Hector.
That's my point. So check. My. Box.

                    HECTOR
You are a fucking lunatic, you know
that? If I weren't a gentleman, I'd
punch you right in the tits. How dare
you reduce me to a concept? I was nice
to you. I paid for this date with rent
money. I have zero disposable income,
but I took a chance because you seemed
cool. Turns out, you're just a spoiled
white girl with an overactive
imagination who wants excitement
without taking any real risks. Well,
forget it! Hector Ignacio Salazar
JUNIOR, by the way, is not a fetish.
Good evening, Jackie. Perhaps you
should summon a Lyft.

                    JACKIE
Disappointing. You can't blame a girl
for trying.

                    HECTOR
Uh, yeah, I can.

JACKIE
Okay, I get that anything long term is
out, but how about I give you a handie
and you show me what's on your butt?

HECTOR
Go!

PREGGO

INT. OFFICE - DAY

MR. CARLISLE CONCLUDES A JOB INTERVIEW WITH
A NINE-MONTH PREGNANT LILA. HE'S HOLDING A
CLIPBOARD WITH HER RESUME. IT'S AWKWARD.

                 MR. CARLISLE
     Well, you're certainly the most
     qualified candidate I've met so far,
     Lila.

                 LILA
     I appreciate that very much.

                 MR. CARLISLE
     Whole Foods would be lucky to have
     someone with your background running
     our Seafood Processing & Distribution
     Center.

                 LILA
     It's not every girl who graduated from
     Vassar with honors and grew up on a
     fishing boat.

                 MR. CARLISLE
     No. (THEN) No, it's not.

                 LILA
     What a weird, perfect fit, huh? I also
     speak Spanish, French and a little
     Somali. I don't know if you saw -

SHE REFERS TO HER RESUME.

MR. CARLISLE

I saw that. That's great. (THEN)
Lila... I think I've asked you all
the questions I'm allowed to ask you,
so... is there anything you'd like to
throw out there?

LILA

Yes. I'm very impressed that you're in
this position at such a young age.

MR. CARLISLE

Oh, thank you. Actually, I was talking
about... you know.

LILA

Nope, I sure don't.

MR. CARLISLE

You're um... Well, the law prohibits
me from asking certain questions in a
job interview, and...

HE STARES AT HER BELLY.

LILA

It should! Some things are private.
That's why I'm not on Facebook. No
goofy party pictures of this girl on
the internet. Not that I don't party,
because I do.

MR. CARLISLE

You do?

                    LILA
          Yes. Privately.

                    MR. CARLISLE
          I guess what I'm trying to say is that
          I'd need to hire someone who could
          start right away.

                    LILA
          I'm looking to start right away.

                    MR. CARLISLE
          And work fulltime.

                    LILA
          I'm your girl.

                    MR. CARLISLE
          Possibly overtime.

                    LILA
          Done.

                    MR. CARLISLE
          And won't need any time off at all in
          the near future!

                    LILA
          Sign me up!

                    MR. CARLISLE
          Lila! I feel you're being disingenuous
          with me regarding your potential
          commitment to the Whole Foods
          Corporation and I'm becoming
          increasingly confused and more than

          MR. CARLISLE (CONT'D)
just a teensy bit angry about it!

LILA STARTS BAWLING LUCY STYLE.

          MR. CARLISLE (CONT'D)
Oh God, please don't.

          LILA
I'm pregnant. You caught me.

          MR. CARLISLE
It wasn't hard. (THEN) You're very
pregnant.

          LILA
I'm nine months pregnant. My water
might break on the way to the car.
I'm so sorry I wasted your time, Mr.
Carlisle. You're so handsome and nice.
And I'm a terrible, lying, hormonal
career monster. I don't blame you for
hating me.

          MR. CARLISLE
I don't hate you at all. I just don't
understand... anything about the last
fourty five minutes.

          LILA
I didn't really expect to get the
job. I just wanted to feel like I
was in the game one last time before
motherhood. I'm going to stay at home
with the baby for a while and I guess
I'm still nervous about "having it

                    LILA (CONT'D)
all." I want to think I can, but I
don't think I can. It's overwhelming!

                    MR. CARLISLE
Ah. That's pretty big stuff. Honestly,
I'm not well-versed in handling lady
troubles.

                    LILA
Nor should you be. You're nineteen
with a job a forty-year-\old should
have.

                    MR. CARLISLE
I'm twenty-nine.

                    LILA
You're adorable. I'm going to take my
big belly and my great big boobs and
go home. I'm sorry for wasting your
time.

                    MR. CARLISLE
No problem. It was nice meeting you
anyway.

                    LILA
You too. Nice interview, kid. Good
questions. You were tough but fair.

                    MR. CARLISLE
I would have hired you if you were,
you know... able to work.

                    LILA
I know. I'm amazing.

                    MR. CARLISLE
And you'll be an amazing mother.

                    LILA
Uh-huh. Oh, just to give you a heads
up, your next interview is a blind
Canadian guy with green card issues.

                    MR. CARLISLE
Great.

SOCIAL

INT. PHOTO BOOTH - NIGHT

BRUCE AND CHLOE HAVE POPPED INTO AN INSTANT
PHOTO BOOTH ON THE BOARDWALK. BRUCE SHOVES
DOLLARS INTO THE MONEY SLOT.

                    BRUCE
          Now let's do one with a crazy face!

                    CHLOE
          Okay, but this is like the forty-fifth
          picture we've taken and I think other
          people are waiting for the booth -

                    BRUCE
          One, two, three... CRAZY FACE!

THEY BOTH MAKE CRAZY FACES AND THE FLASH
GOES OFF.

                    CHLOE
          This was fun Bruce, but I'm going to
          have a seizure if I stare into one
          more flash. Let's go.

                    BRUCE
          No, wait! I want to ask you something.

                    CHLOE
          Okay. Can you ask me outside the photo
          booth?

                    BRUCE
          I can, but I like it in here. Confined
          spaces help me with my spacial
          ambiguity disorder.

                    CHLOE
Right. I forget infinity terrifies
you... So?

                    BRUCE
Well, we've been seeing each other a
while now.

                    CHLOE
Oh, God. You're not proposing to me in
a photo booth are you?

                    BRUCE
What? No. What am I, a Kardashian?

                    CHLOE
Sorry, it sounded like you were
winding up.

                    BRUCE
I was, but not for that. One step at
a time. And I think the next step is
a social media acknowledgment of our
profound love and deep commitment to
each other.

                    CHLOE
Like a Facebook post?

                    BRUCE
And an update of our relationship
status on all of our online profiles:
Twitter, Instagram, Snapchat, LinkedIn
for me, even though you think it's
stupid, Pinterest for you, even though
I think it's stupid... Chloe Bennett,

> BRUCE (CONT'D)
> will you be my - as searchable on the
> internet - "in a relationship with"
> significant other?

> CHLOE
> Sure. Should we do that right now on
> our phones, or...?

BRUCE IS STUNNED AND STUMBLES FOR WORDS.

> BRUCE
> Well, uh, we could do that, or...

> CHLOE
> You want us to take a picture doing
> it?

> BRUCE
> No!

> CHLOE
> Then what do you want?

> BRUCE
> I want you to care! I want you to get
> excited and jump into my arms and
> kiss me because I just asked you to
> take an important next step in our
> relationship.

> CHLOE
> Oh, sweetie, that's lame, so, no.

> BRUCE
> Lame?!

                    CHLOE
Yeah. I see why you'd think it was
cool, but it's not cool, so let's just
grab our pictures and find a frozen
margarita place. My ass is sore from
this booth bench.

                    BRUCE
Informing your social network of
life's milestones is a valid part of
our culture now, Chloe.

                    CHLOE
I didn't say it wasn't valid, it's
just not my thing.

                    BRUCE
Huh. You know, I'm really not
sure what the point is in having a
girlfriend if no one knows about it.

                    CHLOE
The people who are important to us
know we're together, Bruce!

                    BRUCE
Everyone we interact with online is
important, Chloe!

                    CHLOE
Are you nuts?

                    BRUCE
No, I am not nuts! I think that since
we live our lives immersed in social
media, it's imperative that

                    BRUCE (CONT'D)
couples successfully navigate moments
of this sort in order to address a
future that will play out in status
updates, tweets, photos, funny memes
and incredibly short videos, as well
as real-life encounters. That's how
not nuts I am!

                    CHLOE
What are you so upset about? I said
I'd do it!

                    BRUCE
Yeah, without any romance!

                    CHLOE
Status updates aren't romantic!

                    BRUCE
Not with that attitude!

                    CHLOE
Okay, we're done. Goodbye, Bruce. I
will find another way home.

                    BRUCE
Wait! I just wanted us to share our
feelings for each other with the
world. What did I say wrong?

                    CHLOE
Everything after, "Do you want to hop
into this photo booth?"

CHLOE EXITS.

                    BRUCE
          Okay, well... guess what my next post
          is about!

TYPES INTO HIS PHONE.

SPLIT

INT. PRICE HOUSE - AFTERNOON

RAMONA, INDIGNANT, WEARING SEDUCTIVE
LINGERIE WITH A LACE WRAP SITS ON THE SOFA.
ARTHUR IS LIVID, HE YELLS OUT THE FRONT
DOOR. HE IS DRESSED IMPECCABLY.

THERE IS A CAKE ON THE COFFEE TABLE IN
FRONT OF THE SOFA.

                    ARTHUR
          - and if I ever catch you in my bed
          again, it'll be the last bed you ever
          lay in except your coffin, you scrawny
          little beaver-faced, hipster dweeb!

                    RAMONA
          It's not your bed anymore, Arthur. And
          you could have given him his clothes.

                    ARTHUR
          Oh really, Ramona?! Is that how we're
          playing this?

                    RAMONA
          Hey! The divorce is almost final and
          you don't live here. It was completely
          inappropriate for you to barge in
          unannounced and flip out like that!

                    ARTHUR
          You are screwing our son's best
          friend! That is inappropriate.

                    RAMONA
          Don't be dramatic.

ARTHUR
Excuse me, Ramona, but when you look
up the definition of inappropriate
in the dictionary, it isn't "Arthur
stopping by the house he paid for to
pick up some important documents to
do his taxes as a single person for
the first time in forever." No, uh-
uh, it's "Ramona rockin' the Casbah
at three-thirty in the afternoon with
Dennis Delgado, who we have all known
since he was five," for Christ's
sake! Look it up, Ramona! That's how
Webster's defines "inappropriate."
God DAMN it, this is disappointing
and weird.

RAMONA
Don't judge me, you pompous asshat!
I cannot stand you when you get
all sanctimonious. As smart as you
are, Arthur, you never learned that
sometimes it's better to be nice than
right. Do you know that you're not
nice? Do you even care?

ARTHUR
I am too nice.

RAMONA
No, you're not.

ARTHUR
Shut up. I'm the nicest fucking guy
you'll ever meet. And don't turn this
around on me, Mrs. Robinson.

                    RAMONA
        Okay, maybe Dennis isn't the best
        choice for rebound sex -

                    ARTHUR
        - maybe?! Is he even eighteen?!

                    RAMONA
        (CAUGHT) Today's his birthday...

                    ARTHUR
        Oh my God!! Is that why there's cake?!

                    RAMONA
        Fine, he's definitely not the best
        choice!

                    ARTHUR
        Thank you.

                    RAMONA
        I haven't dated anyone in two decades,
        Arthur. I don't know how to do it and
        I don't know any single people. I
        know... Dennis.

                    ARTHUR
        Biblically, now. I mean, this did
        start after we decided - ?

                    RAMONA
        Of course. Don't be ridiculous. I
        wouldn't cheat on you with a child.

                    ARTHUR
        What does that mean?

                    RAMONA
What?

                    ARTHUR
You wouldn't cheat on me with a
child... would you cheat on me with an
adult?

                    RAMONA
Are you serious?

                    ARTHUR
Yes, I'm serious. Separating has
been hard on me too, you know! I have
feelings, Ramona, real insecurities.

                    RAMONA
You are the most selfish person I have
ever met! Do you know how difficult
you are?

                    ARTHUR
I just asked a question!

                    RAMONA
Arthur, I didn't cheat on you with
anybody. Ever! (THEN) Did you cheat on
me?

                    ARTHUR
Can we please just leave the past in
the past?

                    RAMONA
Are you fucking kidding me?

ARTHUR
This isn't going to help anything!

RAMONA
Who, Arthur? WHEN??

ARTHUR
I don't want to discuss this.

RAMONA
Too late!

ARTHUR
Alright! I'll tell you, but you're
going to try and spin this like we're
even, but we're not even, because I
SAW this.

RAMONA
Tell me or I'll punch you in the
throat. I've been taking Krav Maga.

ARTHUR
I made out with Angela Bauman at an
open house three weeks before I moved
out. She was helping me find a new
place and we got carried away in the
kitchen pantry while an unrelated
young couple was looking at the master
bedroom. It was uncharacteristically
risqué on my part, and I'm not proud
of myself.

RAMONA
That's it? You made out with our real
estate agent friend in a big cupboard?

ARTHUR
That was it.

RAMONA
Angela and Dan are still married,
Arthur. You kissed a married woman.

ARTHUR
But you didn't see it.

RAMONA
Alright. So, are you two -

ARTHUR
No, no. It was a heat of the moment
thing. She felt sorry for me. They've
been going through some stuff...
Perhaps we were standing too close to
the spice rack.

RAMONA
Honestly, this might sound crummy, but
I'm kind of glad.

ARTHUR
How so?

RAMONA
I'm glad I'm not the only one who's
messed up. Angela and Dan run around
town like they're Mr. and Mrs.
Perfect. If they've got problems I'm
sure everyone else around here does,
too. God knows you're a disaster. To
tell you the truth, I'm feeling better
about some of my recent choices.

ARTHUR
Predictable. Using other people's
misery to justify your illicit affair.

RAMONA
Don't psychoanalyze me, Arthur. It
makes me want to day drink. Dennis is
cute.

ARTHUR
He has a man-bun.

RAMONA
Would you like some cake, Arthur?

ARTHUR
Is this a pretense to try and get me
to move back in?

RAMONA
Center piece or corner?

ARTHUR
You know I hate the corner piece.
You're only asking to antagonize me.

RAMONA
Have cake or go.

ARTHUR
Center piece, but not the one with his
fucking name on it. Dweeb.

STRIPETEASE

INT. HOSPITAL ROOM - DAY

OPEN ON DEAN YANK LAID UP IN A HOSPITAL
BED. BELINDA ENTERS, YELLING AT A NURSE
DOWN THE HALL.

> BELINDA
> I can't be fired. I'm a volunteer. If
> I don't get a written apology, you'll
> be sorry you ever laid eyes on Belinda
> Sue Titus. Ah, kiss my ass!

THEIR EYES MEET AND THERE IS AN INSTANT
ATTRACTION.

> DEAN
> Hello, luscious. You're a slice of
> heaven.

> BELINDA
> We've already met. You were
> unconscious. I was out on the tarmac
> having a smoke when the helicopter
> brought you in. What's your name?

> DEAN
> Dean Yank. And you are...

> BELINDA
> Belinda Sue Titus.

> DEAN
> So, what's your story, pussycat?

> BELINDA
> I've been a candystriper here at

BELINDA (CONT'D)
Mothers of Mercy for twenty-seven and
a half years. I don't get paid cause
I'm a volunteer, but that's alright...
I'm on welfare.

DEAN
I admire your drive.

BELINDA
It's nothin'. I just like being around
sick people. So, Dean... tell me
what's wrong with ya' and I'll tell
you what's in my happy cart.

DEAN
Deal! I'm on location here in
Gainesville shooting a new flick...

BELINDA
You're a celebrity, huh?

DEAN
I'm a stunt man, for kids.

BELINDA
Even better.

DEAN
So, I'm standing in for the fat kid on
"Stranger Things." They made the whole
series for a nickel.

BELINDA
(WE HEAR A BEEP) Excuse me, I'm
getting beeped. (OUT THE DOOR) Would

                    BELINDA (CONT'D)
you nurses quit paging me? Excuse
me...

                    DEAN
So one of those goddamn creatures
starts coming for me and he's drunk. A
lot of us are major alcoholics. He has
a PTSD flashback and all of his stunt
etiquette goes out the window. He just
goes nuts! He starts wailing on me
while tiny, but surprisingly strong,
Winona Ryder does her best to pull him
off. The next thing I know, I've got
major organ displacement. My spleen
got shoved up right under my heart
and my intestines are all wrapped up
around my lungs.

                    BELINDA
Yeah. I saw you when they brought you
in. Your kidney was hangin' out your
ass.

                    DEAN
Is that what it was?

                    BELINDA
Yeah. Mind if I smoke?

                    DEAN
No. Mind if I watch?

                    BELINDA
I'd let you have one, but the doc says
it's bad for you.

                    DEAN
         Maybe I'll just have a little
         secondhand.

BELINDA TAKES A DRAG OF HER CIGARETTE AND
BLOWS THE SMOKE DIRECTLY INTO DEAN'S MOUTH.

                    BELINDA
         So... can I whip you up some potatoes?

                    DEAN
         Mmmmmmm... comfort food. That would
         hit the spot right about now. But I
         don't want you out of my sight.

                    BELINDA
         I'm not going anywhere, Tiger.
         Belinda's bedside cuisine is brought
         fresh to you.

SHE PULLS OUT HER HOT PLATE WITH A POT,
THE SPUDS AND A CUP OF WATER. SHE STARTS
MIXING.

                    DEAN
         You're just a jack-of-all trades,
         aren't you?

                    BELINDA
         And unlike most people, I'm a master
         of all of them. I'm just gonna let
         these boil.

                    DEAN
         Belinda, you flirtin' with me?

BELINDA
Maybe. But I'm playin' it close to the
vest. I've been hurt before.

DEAN
Who did this to you, cupcake? Give me
a name and I'll take care of him. I
know people.

BELINDA
Just some Joe who came in with
frostbite. They released him a couple
of days ago and he hasn't called. But
I keep his toe on a chain.

DEAN
Well, I'm not him.

BELINDA
Oh, this is moving too fast! My heart
says stay, but my legs say run!

DEAN
We can take it slow, candy cane, I'm
here for a week.

BELINDA
A location romance? I don't know if
I'm up for that. (PULLS OUT A BOTTLE
AND TAKES A SWIG) Touch me in the
morning, then just walk away.

DEAN
I'm not leavin' you, Belinda. When I
go back to Barstow I want you with me.
I gotta junior one bedroom in the

DEAN (CONT'D)
prettiest little trailer park you've
ever seen. Help me make it a home.

BELINDA
Will you be a good daddy to our kids?

DEAN
You bet, I'm around kids all the time.
I know how to make 'em laugh, keep 'em
in line, take a fall for 'em if I have
to.

BELINDA
Good. I got one good egg left, and I
want it to go to a man I can trust.

DEAN
I'm not gonna leave you with nothin'
but a toe to remember me by.

BELINDA
You got yourself a deal, Mr. Yank.

THEY BOTH SPIT INTO PALMS AND THEN SHAKE.

DEAN
You're gonna make one pretty bride,
Belinda.

BELINDA
You too. I gotta go hold some preemies
in neonatal intensive care.

DEAN
Don't go gettin' yourself too attached.

                    BELINDA
          They need me.

                    DEAN
          So do I!

                    BELINDA
          I'll be back as soon as I can.

                    DEAN
          Leave the spuds.

SHE HANDS HIM THE POT.

                    BELINDA
          When I return, maybe I can find out a
          little something about you.

                    DEAN
          Like what?

                    BELINDA
          Got a middle name?

                    DEAN
          Yeah. It's Laurel. All that and more
          is waitin' for ya'!

                    BELINDA
          I'm not usually an open book, but I'll
          let you thumb through my pages.

                    DEAN
          Godspeed!

SHE EXITS.

                    BELINDA
          Hey, you! Medicine man! I'm not gonna
          tell you again... give me back what's
          mine.

                    DEAN
          (TAKES A SNIFF, THEN A BITE OF THE
          POTATOES) You're a lucky man, Dean
          Yank!

SURVIVOR

INT. JULIA'S OFFICE - DAY

JULIA IS AT THE DOORWAY FAKING A NICE
GOODBYE TO HER ARCHRIVAL TABITHA THORENSEN,
WHO IS EXITING DOWN THE HALL.

DERRICK, HER FAITHFUL ASSISTANT, IS WAITING
NEARBY FUMING ON JULIA'S BEHALF.

>   JULIA
> Take care, darling. It's always a
> delight to have you drop by. Ta!

SHE TURNS BACK INTO HER OFFICE.

>   JULIA (CONT'D)
> God, I hate that woman!

>   DERRICK
> I hate her more!

>   JULIA
> How dare she walk in here unannounced?

>   DERRICK
> How dare she?!

>   JULIA
> She wants my job, Derrick!

>   DERRICK
> Which is absurd because you are
> irreplaceable!

>   JULIA
> I am the only female president of a

                    JULIA (CONT'D)
major film studio in Hollywood and she
wants to take me out! How about going
after one of the men who grease the
wheels of this shit town?

                    DERRICK
How about it, huh?!

                    JULIA
If it weren't for me, Tabitha
Thorensen would be a great big nobody!

                    DERRICK
Nobody at all! First of all, she's
named after a fictitious witch. Second
of all, she's an actual witch. Third
of all, I think we should be a little
worried because she just won an Oscar
and her last film grossed over a
billion dollars.

                    JULIA
I don't worry, Derrick. It does mean
things to a woman's face.

                    DERRICK
You are delicious. Revenge it is.
I'll formulate a plan and we will
retaliate. I can have a fully realized
smear campaign ready by 2:30.

                    JULIA
No, Derrick.

                    DERRICK
Oh, my God. We're not going to Defcon
5, are we? I mean, we've talked
about... eliminating people before.
I'll need more time if we're going to
"call our friend in Mexico."

                    JULIA
No, we're not going to feed her corpse
to the desert, either. Believe me, I'd
love nothing more...

                    DERRICK
Are we quitting?

                    JULIA
Have you met me?

                    DERRICK
Okay, I'm lost. We have outlined
detailed scenarios for every
eventuality that involves you losing
your job. Our acute awareness that
you are Hollywood's biggest target is
exactly what's kept you safe for the
last seventeen years!

                    JULIA
Safe? You're hilarious.

                    DERRICK
Julia, we are the gatekeepers of the
entire global entertainment system.

                    JULIA

We were, Derrick. Somebody just
changed the lock. Tabitha's the real
deal. She's smart. She's talented.
She's a thirty-six year old lesbian
who shits money. She's in the ether.
She's what the industry wants. I can't
stop that. I'm just an extraordinarily
strong straight woman with a fanatical
gay executive assistant. That played
us this far down the fairway, but I
think we just sliced ourselves into
a double bogey. And now it's time to
head back to the clubhouse, knock back
a bourbon and call it a day.

                    DERRICK

You've never... used an extended golf
metaphor before. Are we going to take
our own lives? Like the Egyptians?

                    JULIA

No, but thank you for remembering
that's in your contract. I'm going to
destroy the studio, Derrick.

                    DERRICK

Mmmmm. A planned demolition. I like
it. Explosives never even occurred to
me!

                    JULIA

Not physically! I'm going to
greenlight it to death. How many bad
scripts do we read in a year?

> DERRICK
> Well, they're all bad. The good
> writers work in TV.

> JULIA
> Fair. But what were the really
> terrible ones? You know, bad grammar,
> improper punctuation, sophomoric
> themes?

> DERRICK
> Well, let's see. There was "Showdogs:
> A Bark Above!"

> JULIA
> The one where the humans were only
> shot from the waist down. Christ,
> that was dreadful. We're gonna make
> it.

> DERRICK
> Nicki Minaj said she'd play the lead
> dog.

> JULIA
> Perfect. What was that one about the
> guy who invented the Snuggie?

> DERRICK
> It was just called "Snuggie."

> JULIA
> That's a go.

> DERRICK
> Oh, I know! There was that German

                    DERRICK (CONT'D)
couple who wrote that three hundred-
page screenplay about the origin of
kindergarten.

                    JULIA
Claus and Magda! God, they were
grim. And that title just made me
uncomfortable...

          DERRICK   JULIA (CONT'D)
Soft Entry.   Soft Entry.

                    DERRICK
Yuck.

                    JULIA
I mean, I get it, when you know it's
about starting school, but when you
first hear it, no thank you.

                    DERRICK
Put it on the list?

                    JULIA
Yes. The American public thinks it's
seen some pretty awful movies over the
last twenty years. They have no idea
what we've actually been protecting
them from.

                    DERRICK
(MOCKING) "So many superheroes,
nothing original, why do they keep
remaking Planet of the Apes?"

                    JULIA
Babies.

                    DERRICK
Well... I've got some calls to make.
It's been an honor working beneath
you, Julia.

                    JULIA
The view from down there must be
spectacular. Thank you, Derrick. I
couldn't have asked for better. Now
let's fuck this place up and... well,
probably never see each other again.

                    DERRICK
I want to eat you up in one bite like
a cake pop.

DERRICK EXITS, VERY DRAMATICALLY...

                    DERRICK (CONT'D)
I TOLD MYSELF I WOULDN'T CRY!

TEACHABLE

INT. CLASSROOM - DAY

KURT SITS ACROSS FROM ELISE AT HER DESK,
ARMS CROSSED. ELISE ATTEMPTS TO REASON WITH
A BEGRUDGING KURT REGARDING HIS SIX YEAR
OLD SON, SCOTTY.

                    ELISE
          I know it must be hard raising a child
          on your own -

                    KURT
          Don't pity me.

                    ELISE
          I'm sure Scotty's... confused -

                    KURT
          Don't pity him.

                    ELISE
          Okay.

ELISE SUMMONS ALL HER PATIENCE.

                    ELISE (CONT'D)
          I've tried various approaches in the
          classroom with Scotty, but he's -

                    KURT
          An asshole. I know, I've met him.

                    ELISE
          WOULD YOU PLEASE STOP CUTTING ME OFF?!

KURT
Sorry. You were saying...

ELISE
I was going to say... difficult.

KURT
Same thing! He's lashing out because
he's angry that his mother just up
and left us and I don't blame him!
He's angry, I'm angry, you're angry.
Everyone's angry except Vanessa
because she's somewhere in the Smoky
Mountains living in a log mansion with
a B-level country singer named Clint
something.

ELISE
Kurt, I am not angry, I am trying to
help.

KURT
How?

ELISE
By... talking to you.

KURT LOOKS AT HER INCREDULOUSLY. HIS EYES
SAY, "REALLY?"

ELISE (CONT'D)
There is an issue with Scotty's
language and behavior. I asked you to
meet me in person. You're here, we're
talking it through...

KURT STARES ON. ELISE SCRAMBLES FOR A NEW
TACTIC.

                    ELISE (CONT'D)
At least one of us is invested in a
solution. (BEAT) Can you please get
your damn kid some therapy so I can
have a break?!

                    KURT
Aha! Angry!

                    ELISE
No, Kurt, I am frustrated. Let me
help.

                    KURT
You can't. That's the point. You can
try, but trying's not helping. Helping
is helping. Trying is wasting my time
and making me feel worse about this
than I already do. You think I haven't
thought of therapy? He goes three
times a week.

                    ELISE
And?

                    KURT
Would you like to see the dolls he
stabbed or the dolls he put in the
toaster?

                    ELISE
Oh.

> KURT

I'm sorry this is landing in your lap.
I know it's affecting you, too. It's
just that everyone I know wants to
talk to me about Scotty and –

> ELISE

No one can actually do anything to
help. Okay, I get it.

THEY SHARE A MOMENT. KURT HAS A FLASH OF
RELIEF. SOMEONE FINALLY GETS IT.

> ELISE (CONT'D)

You're dismissed.

> KURT

Excuse me?

> ELISE

Dismissed.

> KURT

That's a little abrupt, isn't it?

> ELISE

No, I don't think so. Goodbye.

> KURT

What are you doing?

> ELISE

Nothing. You've made one simple point
since you sat down here and it took me
a while to get it. I can't help you.
What else is there to say?

                    KURT
          Well, what about Scotty?

                    ELISE
          I don't know. He's got one decent
          parent, he's seeing a counselor. I'll
          do what I can.

                    KURT
          That's it?

                    ELISE
          Yep.

                    KURT
          I don't know if I like your attitude.

                    ELISE
          What attitude? I saw the light, Kurt.
          He's your kid, I'm following your
          lead.

                    KURT
          (DUMBFOUNDED) Are you mirroring me?

ELISE PRETENDS TO HOLD A FRAME AROUND HER
FACE AND STARES AT KURT.

                    ELISE
          Look familiar?

                    KURT
          Well, quit it. I don't like it!

                    ELISE
          Are you angry?

                    KURT
I'm getting there!

                    ELISE
Why? Because I'm throwing up my hands
and giving up on Scotty?

                    KURT
Yes!

                    ELISE
Like you're doing?

                    KURT
What?!

                    ELISE
You think someone helping you is
having them solve the problem all
at once, and that isn't going to
happen. The people who care about you
and Scotty are going to have to try
and fail to fix this before it gets
better. Newsflash, Dad! No one trying
is very quickly going to turn into no
one caring. Now dismiss yourself.

KURT IS THOROUGHLY SCHOOLED. HE TAKES A
MOMENT TO REEVALUATE HIS POINT OF VIEW.

                    KURT
Did you just... teach me something?

                    ELISE
I don't know. Did I?

KURT DOES HIS BEST TO RESET.

>   KURT
>   Is there anything you can suggest that
>   might help Scotty manage his feelings
>   better while he is at school?

SHE PULLS OUT A STACK OF BOOKS.

>   ELISE
>   Uh, yeah. You think this is my first
>   problem child? Every other kid in this
>   class is a reality show in the making.

KURT LAUGHS.

>   ELISE (CONT'D)
>   Don't laugh.

>   KURT
>   Oh.

ELISE PROCEEDS TO ADVISE HIM WITH THE
READING MATERIAL.

>   ELISE
>   Now, here's the first thing you should
>   read...

UNSLUMP

INT. BEDROOM - NIGHT

ADAM CLIPS HIS TOENAILS IN BED AS KATE
READS A MAGAZINE NEXT TO HIM.

                    ADAM
          We haven't had sex in a long time.

                    KATE
          Mmm-hmm.

                    ADAM
          I think it's been like three weeks or
          something.

                    KATE
          It's been a while.

                    ADAM
          Well, do you care?

                    KATE
          Oh, I care. I care a lot. I'm so horny
          I licked a picture of Hugh Jackman's
          chest a minute ago when you went to
          the bathroom.

                    ADAM
          Well then, why haven't we had sex in
          three weeks?

                    KATE
          Maybe it's because you clip your
          toenails in our bed.

HE LOOKS AT THE CLIPPERS, THEN PUTS THEM
ASIDE.

> ADAM
> Seriously, what's the real reason
> we're not having sex?

> KATE
> That's pretty much it. You have
> disgusting habits that make you super
> unsexy.

> ADAM
> Harsh.

> KATE
> Sorry, that was a little in your face.
> You say something about me that's not
> sexy.

> ADAM
> Really?

> KATE
> Oh, God no, I'd punch you right in the
> neck.

> ADAM
> Do you want to have sex right now?

> KATE
> Not really. Do you?

> ADAM
> No.

                    KATE
I'm licking magazines and you treat
our bed like a dumpster. Is there
something wrong with us?

                    ADAM
We're in a slump.

                    KATE
Well, we have to unslump. I don't want
to never have sex with you again, even
though I don't particularly want to
have sex with you right now.

SILENCE.

                    ADAM
Maybe we should force ourselves.

                    KATE
What, force sex on each other?

                    ADAM
Yeah. Maybe if we force it, we'll get
into it.

                    KATE
Mutual rape.

                    ADAM
It's not rape if it's mutual.

                    KATE
True. So... how should we start?
Should I hit you? Do you want to pull
my hair?

ADAM

No, I like your hair. It's beautiful.

KATE

Oh, Adam. I just got a little tingle
in my jelly jar.

ADAM

Have I ever told you how beautiful
your eyes are, even though they're not
quite the same size?

KATE

I can't believe you look at them that
closely.

ADAM

Maybe all we needed was a little sweet
talk to get things going.

KATE

Well, mister, keep talking.

ADAM

I like that you only have one dimple
and your breath smells like green tea.

THEY EMBRACE. ADAM BECOMES CLEARLY AROUSED.

KATE

Oh, Adam. You're not slumping anymore!

FEMALE & FEMALE SCENES

BAKED

INT. ANNETTE'S KITCHEN - AFTERNOON

ANNETTE AND LANIE ARE ARGUING OVER A
WEDDING CAKE.

> ANNETTE
> I swear to God, Lanie, if you don't
> put that spatula down, you're a dead
> woman.

> LANIE
> Someone has got to save this cake,
> Annette!

> ANNETTE
> Yes. And as the resident pastry chef,
> that would be me!

> LANIE
> You're too close to it! There must
> be twelve pounds of frosting on this
> thing. And it's buttercream! Are you
> trying to bless their wedding day
> or clog their arteries before the
> honeymoon?

> ANNETTE
> It tastes good, Lanie! And Melissa and
> Mike asked me to make it for them!
> So either back away, or there will be
> consequences. I have a Cuisinart.

> LANIE
> Now you're threatening me? My God,
> woman, listen to yourself!

ANNETTE
Step away, Lanie! Quit cake-blocking
me!

LANIE
Annette, you're not a pastry chef!
You're in cooking school. Melissa
and Mike both just lost their jobs,
didn't want to delay their wedding and
asked for a free cake! That's the only
reason you're doing this.

ANNETTE
So I clearly have something to prove.
I know it's not perfect. The frosting
covers some of the mistakes. Do you
think it's supposed to be shaped
like a hexagon? No. Do you think the
flowers are supposed to look like cat
tongues? No. The cake has problems. I
get it!

LANIE
Then let me help. You're losing your
perspective on this.

ANNETTE
I have to do this alone!

LANIE
What's the big deal?

ANNETTE
It's my job.

                         LANIE
          And...?

                        ANNETTE
          It's my only job, Lanie.

                         LANIE
          I don't get it.

                        ANNETTE
          I'm not in the wedding party. I'm the
          only one of us Melissa didn't ask to
          be in the wedding.

                         LANIE
          Oh. Sorry. I didn't think you'd be
          into all that bridesmaid stuff. I
          guess Melissa didn't either.

                        ANNETTE
          Yeah, well... I guess that's what
          happens when you go around saying
          you'll never get married and you think
          weddings make slaves out of women
          stupid enough to have them.

                         LANIE
          Kind of. Do you really believe that?

                        ANNETTE
          I do. But, believe it or not, I still
          want to be there for my friends if
          they don't. Melissa and Mike are
          perfect together. And I really wanted
          to make them a perfect cake to show
          them how happy I am for them.

LANIE
Well, perfect's off the table.

ANNETTE
Yeah. (THEN) I'm sorry I threatened to kill you with an appliance.

LANIE
Accepted.

ANNETTE
I guess we should scrape some of this frosting off.

LANIE
Most of it.

ANNETTE
Am I too young to be this cynical about love?

LANIE
Why don't you pour yourself a mug of frosting and we'll talk.

COPIES

<u>INT. COUNSELOR'S OFFICE - AFTERNOON</u>

MS. WANG, AN ASIAN-AMERICAN GUIDANCE
COUNSELOR, IS EXTREMELY POSITIVE AND A BIT
ECCENTRIC. HOLLY IS ACROSS FROM HER DESK,
CLEARLY DISTRAUGHT.

>   MS. WANG
> Oh... okay, don't be upset, Miss
> Lachlin. Here's what we will do...

>   HOLLY
> It's McLachlan.

>   MS. WANG
> We are going to have all the students
> in your class write a letter of
> apology to you. Then the letter will
> go into their files, and you get a
> copy, and I get a copy, which means
> everyone will have a copy, and there
> is a total of THREE copies!

>   HOLLY
> Um... right. And then if they do it
> again?

>   MS. WANG
> Oh, I doubt they'll do it again. So
> many copies...

>   HOLLY
> Ms. Wang. I was totally humiliated.
> They were all playing that video at
> the same time when I walked into the
> classroom... laughing, taunting...

HOLLY (CONT'D)
they called me the white Solange. God,
I hate YouTube!

MS. WANG
Yeah, cameras everywhere these days.
You gotta be careful when you
beat the crap out of your man in
public.

HOLLY
It's not like I planned it. Steve and
I were having our anniversary dinner
at Ruth's Chris Steakhouse. He's a
big meat eater. Anyway, he went to the
bathroom and his phone buzzed on the
table. I never look at it - I just
wanted to silence it so we could eat
in peace and that's when I saw... when
I realized...

MS. WANG
Steve was making bang bang with your
best friend.

HOLLY
You saw it, too?

MS. WANG
It went pretty viral. You beat him
unconscious with a grass-fed rib eye!

HOLLY
Just my luck, TMZ was there because
Justin Bieber was unveiling a new

                    HOLLY (CONT'D)
Pinot Noir he created.

                    MS. WANG
I think they just put his name on it.
That kid's batshit.

                    HOLLY
I know. But anyway, they were there,
I was hitting a grown man with his
dinner, and then, in a blind rage, I
threw a pepper mill at the aquarium,
which cracked open and killed a few
dozen innocent fish...

                    MS. WANG
And that's why you moved here from
Alhambra?

                    HOLLY
Uh-huh. Although, I'm starting to
think I might have made a big mistake
in coming here to teach. Apparently,
I'm just as crazy in Pittsburgh.

                    MS. WANG
You're not crazy. You're just famous
in a horrible way. Things like this
pass. Why don't you stick it out for
a few more days, see what happens? If
the students still give you a hard
time, just send them to me, and we'll
have them sign contracts to behave!
EVERYONE will get copies. You copy, me
copy, parents' copy -

                    HOLLY
Thank you, Ms. Wang. What's your first
name?

                    MS. WANG
Too hard for you to pronounce. You
know, you should talk to Ms. Earnhart,
the biology teacher. She's a lesbian.
She knows what it's like to be an
outcast, so you two get along great.

                    HOLLY
Outcast. Right. Well, tomorrow's a
better day!

                    MS. WANG
If you don't hit anyone with meat,
then it should be. Bye-bye, Holly!

SISTERHOOD

INT. CLASSROOM - DAY

GRACE IS JUST FINISHING READING A FREELANCE
ARTICLE MIA HAS WRITTEN FOR A MAGAZINE.

                    GRACE
          This is...

                    MIA
          Yeah?

                    GRACE
          It's...

                    MIA
          Uh-huh...

                    GRACE
          Offensive in a way that I can't quite
          believe you're not aware of!

                    MIA
          What? No, no, no! It's cute, frothy
          summer reading for the beach.

                    GRACE
          It's everything that's wrong with the
          way women are depicted by the media!
          And you're leading the charge! "How
          to Twist Yourself Up Into a Passion
          Pretzel That Your Man Wants to Take a
          Bite Out Of." What the hell?

                    MIA
          It's just a little advice on how to be
          sexy and appealing. This is what the

MIA (CONT'd)
editors of women's magazines want!

GRACE
Mia, you're a good writer. Fine, if
you need to freelance on the side
to make money, but this? Really?
"Understand the Caveman Inside Him
- Let Him Pull Your Hair Once In a
While."

MIA
Right. Once in a while.

GRACE
Oh, my God! Do you hear yourself? It's
not 1955!

MIA
Oh, stop it. It's not like I'm telling
women to... do whatever you guys did
back in 1955.

GRACE
I wasn't alive in 1955.

MIA
Okay, run with that. I guess that's
why you're the creative writing
teacher. You know girls my age aren't
feminists right?

GRACE
I do and it makes me a little sad.

MIA

Because you're a feminist. You don't
have to be. Maybe if you stopped,
you'd be happy.

GRACE

I AM HAPPY!

MIA

Reeeaarr.

GRACE

Mia, I just think women should support
each other.

MIA

Oh, well I agree with that.

GRACE

Then what do you think feminism is?

MIA

Like anger... or burning your bra
for some weird reason... The lady
version of freeing slaves? I don't
really know. I don't think men like
feminists.

GRACE

Well, a lot of them don't. Why is it
important for men to like you?

MIA

I want everyone to like me. I don't
think I'm getting anywhere with you
though.

GRACE
You're telling women to subjugate
their needs with this garbage.

MIA
Short term. Long term, we get what we
want. You didn't read this the right
way.

GRACE
Excuse me?

MIA
I think you're missing the part where
I make it perfectly clear that all my
suggestions are manipulations to get
men to behave exactly the way you want
them to without them ever knowing what
you're doing, and get exactly what
you need from a relationship without
having to ask for it directly.

GRACE
That's so passive-aggressive!

MIA
It's not passive-aggressive if it
works!

GRACE
It's ONLY passive-aggressive if it
works!

MIA
You are determined to ruin this for me!
What is your deal? Are you jealous?

                    GRACE
No, Mia. I am definitely not jealous.
I am only trying to help my fellow
woman.

                    MIA
Me too.

                    GRACE
Oh, I see. I didn't realize you were a
Gloria Steinem in the making.

                    MIA
Okay, I don't know who that is and I
know you think that makes me stupid,
but I don't care. I'm probably going
to get fifteen hundred bucks for this
article.

                    GRACE
Well, congratulations. But you're
not just selling these words; you're
selling your soul.

                    MIA
Then I'll ask for two thousand.

MIA EXITS. GRACE TAKES A LAST LOOK AT THE
ARTICLE.

                    GRACE
"98 Positions in 36 Days: How to Be
the Sexual Banquet He Wants to Feast
Upon for Every Meal." Ouch. That makes
me sad and sore.

VEGGIE

INT. LIVING ROOM - DAY

DANA AND LIZA SIP ICED TEA OVER A TENSE
CONVERSATION.

> DANA
> So, truth be told, it was Ed's idea
> that I come over and hang.

> LIZA
> Huh. Remind me to thank him.

> DANA
> So I'm thinking you and me spend the
> day together and get to know each
> other. Bestie it up and what not.

> LIZA
> Dana, I'd - oh, my goodness. It's
> time for my archery lesson with Geena
> Davis. I'm so sorry. I must run.

> DANA
> Oh, bomb diggity! I love archery! It's
> so "Game of Thrones." Sometimes I wish
> I had a falcon. How cool would it be
> if we were out on the range with you
> shooting arrows into a target and my
> falcon retrieving them back into your
> quiver?

> LIZA
> Well, I think that would be like
> something out of a cartoon. Ta-ta!

                    DANA
Wait, don't go. Two more minutes.
We're just getting started. (THEN) I
know! We'll play most embarrassing
moment. That's a good ice breaker. You
go first.

                    LIZA
Would I be embarrassed for myself or
on behalf of someone else who didn't
know to be embarrassed for herself? I
feel that way a lot.

                    DANA
I'll go first. Um, so I'm twelve years
old when I find out people actually
eat meat.

                    LIZA
Oh. How embarrassing. Ciao.

                    DANA
No, that's not it. It gets worse. So I
figure, I gotta try it, right? So I go
down to White Castle, and I buy a sack
of sliders. And I'm scarfing them down
out back by the dumpster, and guess
who drives by?

                    LIZA
I can't even imagine.

                    DANA
Come on, guess.

                    LIZA
Really, my mind's eye fails me.

                    DANA
Please...

                    LIZA
I - uh... the meat police.

                    DANA
Well, my mom, so, good guess. Strict
vegan. I was so busted. And then, the
very next day, I got my first period.
So now, in my mind, those two things
are somehow tied together.

                    LIZA
Alright! Game's over, game's over!

                    DANA
Okay, so you don't like me yet, but
one day, in the future, you're going
to like me. And you're going to feel
really bad about not having come to my
party as a favor to your future self.
See, it's the kind of thing that the
you you're going to be will want to
have done for the me that I am now.

                    LIZA
Fine. For family's sake, I will
come to your party. Please know that
finger foods and cover bands are deal
breakers.

                    DANA
That changes the menu and
entertainment portion... but sure!

                    LIZA
And Dana, please - let's neither one
of us have a new most embarrassing
moment when this is done.

                    DANA
I'll try, but let's be real. It's
inevitable.

LIZA EXITS.

MALE & MALE SCENES

BALLERS

INT. RICHARD'S OFFICE - DAY

OPEN ON RICHARD, WHO SITS BEHIND HIS DESK,
ON THE PHONE. HE IS THE PRINCIPAL OF LAKE
TRAVIS HIGH SCHOOL, AUSTIN, TEXAS.

                    RICHARD
         Well, we could do dinner with the
         Martins on Friday, move date night to
         Wednesday and take the twins to the
         planetarium on Saturday, but I'm going
         to have to carve out some alone time
         on Sunday to clear the rain gutters. I
         can't imagine the leaves are going to
         pull themselves out. Well, I find your
         organizational skills equally erotic.
         See you at home.

RICHARD ENDS THE CALL AND GOES BACK TO
WORK ON HIS COMPUTER. BILLY RAY ENTERS,
INFURIATED, HOLDING A FILE OF PAPERWORK.
HE'S WEARING GYM SHORTS, A STRIPED POLO,
TUBE SOCKS, SNEAKERS AND A WHISTLE AROUND
HIS NECK.

                    BILLY RAY
         Pardon me for just barging in,
         Richard, but I have a very big bone to
         pick with you.

                    RICHARD
         That's unfortunate, because I don't -
         what are the kids saying these days...?
         - uhh, give any fucks. Yes, that's it.
         I give zero fucks.

BILLY RAY
You could have at least talked to me
first, you persnickity man-bitch!

RICHARD
But that's the beauty of our
relationship, Billy Ray. I'm the
principal of Lake Travis High School
and you're the gym teacher. Principal
is another word for boss. I don't
think gym teacher has a synonym,
because... why would it? Don't you
have some jockstraps to Lysol?

BILLY RAY
AND FOOTBALL COACH! I'm the gym
teacher and football coach, Dick!
And you just petitioned the school
district to phase out the football
program because one kid got hurt!
What the hell?

RICHARD
Tyler Phelps suffered a dislocated
shoulder and severe concussion.

BILLY RAY
No, duh! I was there, Captain Pansy.
I pulled him from the game and sent
him to the medic. I followed up with
his parents yesterday. Tyler's fine.

RICHARD
As far as we know. Civil cases are
springing up left and right because
young athletes are incurring injuries

RICHARD (CONT'D)
that cause chronic conditions.

BILLY RAY
Lawyers make up reasons to sue people.
It's their job. I believe we're
protected from fake lawsuits by a
little something called the Magna
Carta.

RICHARD
That's not - what? If you'd read a
newspaper every once in a while, you
might have seen this storm's been
brewing, Billy Ray. We finish this
season and next year, the Cavaliers
will transition into a soccer team.

BILLY RAY
SOCCER?! OH MY GOD! Why don't we just
open a gay bar while we're at it? We
live in Texas, Richard. We're kind of
known for high school football. Maybe
you should have watched *Friday Night
Lights* every once in a while.

RICHARD
I did. It was on Wednesdays. That made
no sense.

BILLY RAY
This is because you threw your arm out
senior year, isn't it?

RICHARD
Watch it, sweat stain.

> BILLY RAY

Mmm hmmm. I'm right, aren't I? Mister Goody Goody, Prom King Quarterback, couldn't finish the season because of a torn ligament and now you're taking it out on all future football players for the history of... forever.

> RICHARD

Do you occasionally hear how stupid you are?

> BILLY RAY

I'm an athlete. I have instincts, Richard. And they're never wrong.

> RICHARD

You're wrong.

> BILLY RAY

Really? Because I love what I do and I think you wish you did something else.

RICHARD GOES BERSERK.

> RICHARD

Fuck you, you fuck!

> BILLY RAY

Okay, flag on the field. That took a turn. My bad. You have a weird vein thing happening on your temple, so... take a breath. Sorry.

> RICHARD

Alright, maybe I wish things would

RICHARD (CONT'D)
have gone another way. But I'm not
trying to punish anyone. It's my job
to protect these kids. We know a lot
more about what they're going through
playing this sport than when we were
their age.

BILLY RAY
And we've made a lot of changes to
make the game safer. Better equipment,
we limit the hits they take. I'd
even go for having more players on
the teams. But I can't 'Bend it Like
Beckham', okay? I'd like to keep my
dignity.

RICHARD
Well, I can't exactly unring a bell.

BILLY RAY
I am not asking you to do that, I just
want to keep football.

RICHARD
I mean I've already filed the
paperwork.

BILLY RAY
Oh, no biggie. I'm tight with the
superintendent. We have beers every
Sunday after church and talk about
what a tight ass you are.

RICHARD
No, you don't.

                    BILLY RAY
We do. He does this really funny
impression of you picking pussy
willows and arranging them in a vase,
all fussy and everything. Hilarious.
I'll just tell him to shred your
whatever.

                    RICHARD
Wow. Okay... I guess we're done and,
um, you'll never need to come into my
office again.

                    BILLY RAY
Yeah, it's been a while. (LOOKS
AROUND) I hate it in here. Take care.

BILLY RAY EXITS. RICHARD GOES BACK TO WORK.

BOOKED

INT. HOME OFFICE - AFTERNOON

CLARK AND ANGUS SIT STARING AT A COMPUTER
SCREEN WITH A MIXTURE OF TENSION AND
FRUSTRATION.

                  CLARK
    Maybe this isn't such a good idea.

                  ANGUS
    This is an excellent idea.

                  CLARK
    What do we really know about children?

                  ANGUS
    Are you kidding? We were children.
    We met when we were children. If
    you'd use the part of your brain that
    remembers things instead of being so
    negative, we'd make more progress.

                  CLARK
    Angus, I think there's more to writing
    children's books than just having been
    a child.

                  ANGUS
    Like what?

                  CLARK
    Like knowing how to write. Feeling
    inspired. Having any vague idea of
    what kids are interested in reading
    about...

ANGUS
You are way over complicating this. We have Oscar the Turtle and we know we need to send him on a hero's journey. All we need is the journey and a moral.

CLARK
But all we've come up with so far is that he wants to cross the highway without getting hit by a car because he's so slow.

ANGUS
Journey. Check.

CLARK
Then what's the moral?

ANGUS
I don't know... for every tiny gain, there's tremendous risk.

CLARK
Angus! That's not something we should be teaching children!

ANGUS
The hell it's not! Those kids are going to have to know how to work the stock market someday and they're gonna be kissing Oscar's ass for teaching them you can be annihilated for making one bad move. My parents live in an apartment now because they thought Circuit City was gonna last forever.

                    CLARK
So, you're saying Oscar's not going to
make it across the highway?

                    ANGUS
I don't know. We're not there yet.

                    CLARK
Well, if your analogy is to a volatile
commodities exchange, it would only
make sense for him to get hit by a
runaway semi-truck that no one saw
coming.

                    ANGUS
Now you're talkin'. Kids like crashes.

                    CLARK
I was being facetious.

                    ANGUS
I know, you're always that way. Side
note - it's not an attractive tone. I
think it's still a good direction for
the story, though. We need to finish
and your other ideas sucked.

                    CLARK
That's entirely untrue. Oscar the
bashful turtle who comes 'out of his
shell' is kind of brilliant!

                    ANGUS
No, it's kind of lame. We worked on that
concept for three days and he didn't
poke his head out until page 28.

ANGUS (CONT'D)

You can't have the main character be
headless for half of the book. We're
not gonna get anywhere with that kind
of dipshittery.

CLARK

We could have had his head come out
sooner!

ANGUS

Then he's not really that shy, is he,
Clark? Maybe he's just being coy.
Where's the tension?!

CLARK

Well, I am not writing a children's
book about an unsuspecting turtle who
gets crushed on the highway just for
trying to get to the other side!

ANGUS

Okay! I'll make it a near miss. But
he should at least get caught up in a
gust of wind from the truck zooming
by that hurls him off a cliff or some
shit.

CLARK

You know, when we were kids, I was the
one who told on you for burning ants
with a magnifying glass.

ANGUS

What?! My mom beat my ass for that,
you big narc! And I didn't get Chuck

                    ANGUS (CONT'D)
E. Cheese's for my birthday. She said
little psychos don't deserve parties.

                    CLARK
Yet, you didn't learn. All these years
later and you still have homicidal
tendencies toward animals.

                    ANGUS
Oscar isn't real, Dingus. And I was
six when I cooked those ants.

                    CLARK
There's a through line that I think is
a valid concern!

                    ANGUS
Is there anything you don't overthink?
Jesus, you're uptight for a Mexican!

                    CLARK
What does that mean?

                    ANGUS
It's not racist, your people just
aren't known for it. I'm gonna write
this book myself, Clark.

                    CLARK
Fine!

                    ANGUS
And Oscar's gonna get hit by that
truck!

                    CLARK
          Whatever!

                    ANGUS
          AND I'm changing Oscar's name to
          Clark.

                    CLARK
          Great! (BEAT) I'm telling your mother!

          CLARK DASHES OUT, ANGUS CHASES AFTER HIM.

                    ANGUS
          Get back here, tattletale!

SNAKED

INT. OFFICE - DAY

STAN IS SEATED AT HIS DESK. ARTIE BURSTS
INTO STAN'S OFFICE IN AN OUTRAGE, CLASPING
A MEMO.

               ARTIE
    Stan, what the hell is this about?

               STAN
    Calm down, Artie...

               ARTIE
    I WILL NOT calm down! We work at AIG!
    I will not be treated like a typical
    citizen of the United States of
    America!

               STAN
    Artie, I HAD to put that memo out. It
    doesn't mean anything. Just throw it
    away and pretend like you never saw
    it.

               ARTIE
    Pretend I what?!! I have seen it,
    Stan, and I may as well have stared
    directly into an eclipse because my
    retinas are burning!

               STAN
    Artie, for God's sake, close the door
    before someone hears you.

STAN CROSSES TO CLOSE THE DOOR.

STAN (CONT'D)

You sound like a lunatic. For the love of Ayn Rand, pull yourself together.

ARTIE

Give our bonuses back? Voluntarily?! I need my bonus, Stan. I didn't work this hard to NOT make one hundred and forty-eight million dollars this quarter.

STAN

I know. It's unimaginable how anyone could live on less than that. But, like it or not, we're going to have to tighten our belts.

ARTIE

Tighten our wha - ? (GASPS) That's one of those colloquialisms for cutting back, isn't it?

STAN

(SIGHS) The climate has changed, Artie. And there's an election coming up. We have to deal with "significant bipartisan outrage in Congress."

ARTIE

Well, of course we do. Their fake outrage. That's the script, we all agreed... we claim we can't afford to lose top-tier talent or the consequences levied against America's economy will become intensified and they pretend the companies'

                    ARTIE (CONT'D)
contractual obligation to pay us
prevents them from withholding our
bonuses and their hands are tied. It's
a win-win for everybody!

                    STAN
The public doesn't see it that way
anymore, Artie. They need to make
SOMEBODY in this situation the
scapegoat.

                    ARTIE
I thought that's what unions were for.

                    STAN
We were invisible for so long, but
now... Now they want "transparency"
and "disclosure" and that goddamn
Elizabeth Warren -

THEY GO INTO BIG SIMULTANEOUS MONOLOGUES.

         ARTIE   STAN (CONT'D)
Oh, don't even get   She's ruining
me started. I hate   EVERYTHING! Ronald
Elizabeth Warren.   Reagan made it
I HATE her. I want   all so EASY! Sure
to kill her. Those   Dubya was an
fucking Democrats   idiot, but you
are destroying   could CONTROL him.
my life! I hate   Then we got Obama,
Elizabeth Warren   but Elizabeth's
and both Clintons,   left of him!
especially Hillary   There's no more
and Bernie Sanders   left to go

ARTIE (CONT'D)
and every one of
those tree-hugging
fags that lives in
a blue state!!

STAN (CONT'D)
after her. It's
just left, left,
left, until you've
gone around in a
goddamn circle!

                    ARTIE
Alright, look. Just last week on
Meet the Press, Chuck Todd said the
government cannot just abrogate our
contracts. Americans don't even know
what abrogate means.

                    STAN
But they have finally gotten wise to
what a good corporate ass raping feels
like. And they're pissed. If we don't
dial back our bonuses, they're going
to try to tax them into oblivion. And
they have the votes to pull it off.

                    ARTIE
Oh, so Republicans want to tax us? Why
do I even vote? How could this happen?

                    STAN
We hold over eighty billion dollars
in life insurance policies around the
globe. And that's only a fraction
of our overall revenue. It's become
impossible not to notice. AIG - in one
way or another - affects the lives of
76% of the people ON THE PLANET!

> ARTIE
> I want to make love to you, Stan.
> Right now. On a big pile of money.

> STAN
> Artie, that's very flattering, but I'm
> not gay.

> ARTIE
> Nor am I.

> STAN
> (BEAT) But if I was...

> ARTIE
> Don't say it.

> STAN
> Then I'll say something even more...
> queer. We have 'work' to do.

> ARTIE
> Work? (SPITS) We're not workers. We
> trade on other people's work. We...
> suggest things. We lobby. We're the
> dark whisper that you can't quite hear
> when you're walking to your car and
> you're alone and don't feel safe.

STAN CROSSES AND PUTS A COMFORTING ARM
AROUND ARTIE'S SHOULDER.

> STAN
> That's who we used to be, Artie. And
> it was intoxicating. But we're going
> to have to act like a 'regular'

                    STAN (CONT'D)
company for now or we won't survive.

                    ARTIE
We're too big to fail. They say it on
the cable news networks all the time.

                    STAN
They say it because it's a meme,
Artie. Not because it's true.

                    ARTIE
I suppose change is inevitable, isn't
it, Stan?

                    STAN
Yep.

                    ARTIE
Well, fuck it. I'll change next week.
Tonight I'm buying a Ferrari, a hooker
and an eight ball. You in?

                    STAN
I can't. I already made plans with
the boys from accounting to play ice
hockey using a live kitten as a puck.

                    ARTIE
Oh, superfun. See you on Monday.

                    STAN
Monday's a holiday! Tuesday, you crazy
kid!

SPOILED

INT. TRENT'S BEDROOM - NIGHT

AGENT BANDI, A SECRET SERVICE AGENT, IS
AWKWARDLY CARRYING YOUNG TRENT, WHO IS
INEBRIATED, LOUD AND OBNOXIOUS, THROUGH THE
DOOR. HE'S BALANCING A CUP OF COFFEE AS
WELL. TRENT IS STILL YAMMERING ON TO THE
UNSEEN STAFF OUTSIDE THE DOOR.

> TRENT
>
> I apologize for barfing, Isabel. I did
> not intend to make all that barf! You
> leave that right there and I will get
> it tomorrow. Just hook me up with a
> sponge and a bucket because I don't
> know where those things are. This
> house is very large and I have never
> cleaned it.

> AGENT BANDI
>
> Thank you, Isabel.

AGENT BANDI SITS TRENT DOWN AND THEN THE
COFFEE.

> TRENT
>
> I meant to barf on you because you
> are an ass face, spoil sport.

> AGENT BANDI
>
> Is that what I am?

> TRENT
>
> Yes. I was having a fantastic time
> with a new lady friend and you ruined
> it. Do your people not know how to

                    TRENT (CONT'D)
      have fun, Agent Kamehameha?

BANDI HELPS TRENT OUT OF HIS COAT.

                    AGENT BANDI
      You were in a brothel with a fake ID.
      I'm from Charleston, which you know
      full well, and therefore makes "my
      people" other American citizens, as
      are the Hawaiians. Since... NINETEEN
      FIFTY-NINE! Drink this.

AGENT BANDI HANDS TRENT THE COFFEE. TRENT
DRINKS AS BANDI TALKS INTO HIS EARPIECE.

                    AGENT BANDI (CONT'D)
      The velociraptor is back in the cage.
      I repeat, the velociraptor has been
      caged, over.

HE HEARS THE COMMAND TO STAY WITH TRENT.
FUCK.

                    AGENT BANDI (CONT'D)
      Understood.

                    TRENT
      Ooooh! Is that what I am? A dangerous
      dinosaur?

                    AGENT BANDI
      As a matter of fact -

TRENT POUNCES ON AGENT BANDI FROM BEHIND
AND PRETENDS TO DEVOUR HIM LIKE A
VELOCIRAPTOR. BANDI SIGHS AND RIDES IT OUT,
UNFLINCHING.

> TRENT
> You just got Jurassic Parked! Hey,
> let's watch it. We can Netflix and
> chill.

> AGENT BANDI
> That's not - NO! Trent, get down now.

TRENT DROPS DOWN.

> AGENT BANDI (CONT'D)
> Listen, kid. This is the last time I
> save your ass. Do you understand?

> TRENT
> I didn't ask you for help, Ponch.

PULLS OUT HIS CELL PHONE AND THROWS HIMSELF
ON THE SOFA.

> AGENT BANDI
> First of all, Erik Estrada is of
> Puerto Rican descent. Second, it's
> Agent Bandi to you. Third, you need
> to find something better to do with
> your time than watch reruns of
> *CHiPS* and lastly, you better start
> letting someone help because you're a
> disaster.

                    TRENT
I am the son of the Vice President
of the United States of America, Man
in Black. I can do whatever the Hello
Kitty I want. You will more or less
act as my personal Mary Poppins so
that my career monster parents don't
have to deal with any of my - what do
they call it? - never ending bullshit.
Furthermore, I have unlocked a new
jelly level on Candy Crush.

                    AGENT BANDI
I don't feel sorry for you.

                    TRENT
Good, I fucking hate you! I don't want
your pity, Tonto.

                    AGENT BANDI
I'm not a Comanche.

TRENT GETS SUDDENLY QUEASY.

                    TRENT
Oh, Jiminy Christmas, I think I'm
gonna hurl.

                    AGENT BANDI
Bathroom!

TRENT RUNS OFF.

                    AGENT BANDI (CONT'D)
Trent, I don't know what you're trying
to prove or who you're trying

                    AGENT BANDI (CONT'D)
          to prove it to, but you need to
          start taking care of yourself. Now,
          it's not my place to get involved
          with the families I'm assigned to,
          but I don't want to see you hurt
          yourself or anyone else with this
          reckless behavior. I know your folks
          have been busy since the election.
          Have you tried reaching out to your
          grandparents? (NOTHING) Trent?
          (NOTHING) Trent, did you hear what I
          said?

TRENT COMES BARRELING OUT OF THE BATHROOM
SHOOTING THE CRAP OUT OF AGENT BANDI WITH
A NERF N-STRIKE ELITE RAPIDSTRIKE CS-18
BLASTER, SCREAMING AND LAUGHING HIS ASS
OFF. TOTALLY CAUGHT OFF GUARD, BANDI GOES
INTO FULL SECRET SERVICE BATTLE MODE, PULLS
OUT A REAL GUN AND LEVELS IT AT TRENT.

                    AGENT BANDI (CONT'D)
          Stand down!

TRENT SCREAMS GIRLISHLY IN REAL, IMMEDIATE
TERROR AND THROWS THE NERF GUN.

                    TRENT
          Don't shoot me, I'm a kid!

BANDI IMMEDIATELY HOLSTERS HIS GUN.

                    AGENT BANDI
          Jesus, Trent. I could have killed you!

                    TRENT
Bro, that was a rush!

                    AGENT BANDI
Trent, I am not now and never will be
your bro. Let's clear that up right
now.

                    TRENT
Fair. You're just some guy who's
around me twenty-four hours a day,
who I barely know and I'm guessing is
going to spend the night in my bedroom
tonight. Because that's normal. Is
that about the size of it? Bro?

THAT ALMOST GETS THE BETTER OF HIM.

                    AGENT BANDI
I am doing my job. Not having killed
you yet means I'm doing it well. Keep
pushing and I'll consider a career
change. Get my meaning, bro?

                    TRENT
THAT is fucking intense. I mean, if I
wasn't white and super rich, I would
be intimidated as shit. But the truth
is, there isn't a goddamn thing you
can do to me that wouldn't ruin your
life forever. So really, you're just a
giant, brown empty threat in a suit.

BANDI HANDS TRENT HIS GUN.

> AGENT BANDI
Shoot me.

> TRENT
What?

> AGENT BANDI
Shoot me.

> TRENT
Fuck off. I'm not going to shoot you.

> AGENT BANDI
Why not? You're the angriest person
I've ever met. You keep going this
way, you're going to kill yourself or
someone else. I'd rather it be me. I'm
prepared. C'mon, maybe you'll feel
better. Shoot me.

> TRENT
No.

> AGENT BANDI
Then respect me.

BANDI HOLSTERS THE GUN. TRENT HAS NO MORE
MOVES LEFT.

> TRENT
Thank you.

> AGENT BANDI
For what?

> TRENT
> I dunno... pulling me off a hooker.
> Not ratting me out. The shitty coffee.

> AGENT BANDI
> You're welcome.

> TRENT
> It's my birthday today. Everybody
> forgot.

> AGENT BANDI
> I don't feel sorry for you. And by the
> way, I'm second-generation Indian,
> since you're horrible at accurately
> insulting people's heritage.

> TRENT
> Gotcha. Oh hey, did you hear about the
> guy who overdosed on curry powder?

> AGENT BANDI
> No, I did not.

> TRENT
> He went into a korma. BAM! Gotcha,
> Deepak! I'd say don't have a cow, but
> I know you can't! Two for two!

AGENT BANDI GLARES.

> TRENT (CONT'D)
> Okay, I should probably hit the sack.

GENDER & AGE NEUTRAL SCENES

HYPOTHETICAL

INT. OFFICE - DAY

HADLEY IS DEEP IN THOUGHT WHILE LANE IS
BUSY WORKING. HADLEY INTERRUPTS.

                    HADLEY
          Hey, Lane. Let me ask you something.
          Say you're crossing the street and
          some guy yells at you because you're
          about to be hit by a bus.

                    LANE
          What street?

                    HADLEY
          What's the difference?

                    LANE
          It's a big difference. Is it a
          piddly, little side street or a main
          thoroughfare?

                    HADLEY
          It's just a street. The size doesn't
          matter.

                    LANE
          Size always matters.

                    HADLEY
          Ha ha. Quit being stupid. I'm trying
          to formulate a defense strategy for a
          case I'm assisting on.

                    LANE
          Well, if it's for a case, you should

                    LANE (CONT'D)
be specific.

                    HADLEY
Lane, I'm not trying the case. I'm
fleshing out a theory and I could use
some help.

                    LANE
I am helping you. The devil is in the
details, kid.

                    HADLEY
Alright, fine, fine. (RANDOMLY)
La Cienega. You happy?

                    LANE
I'm emotionally neutral, Hadley, simply
acquiring information. La Cienega is a
major artery running through one of the
biggest cities in the United States of
America. How you thought that wasn't
relevant is beyond me.

                    HADLEY
It's not about the street, Lane!

                    LANE
All variables are a factor. Let's talk
about this guy.

                    HADLEY
Random stranger.

                    LANE
Or is he?

                    HADLEY
Immaterial. His motive is your safety,
whether you know him or not.

                    LANE
Okay, okay. Now we're talkin'. Why am
I in the street?

                    HADLEY
You're an idiot.

                    LANE
Objection!

                    HADLEY
You're crossing it. The walk sign
is white. You're with the flow of
traffic.

                    LANE
Why don't I see the bus myself?

                    HADLEY
Dropped your cell phone.

                    LANE
I could retrieve my phone without
distraction.

                    HADLEY
It was ringing when it fell. Ryan
Reynolds was calling.

                    LANE
My celebrity bro crush. Damn! Alright,
I'm in the street. What about the

LANE (CONT'D)
bus... Is it local or an express?

HADLEY
Who cares? It's orange.

LANE
Well, I need to know how fast it's
going. If it's a local, it might stop
on its own. But if it's an express,
it's just going to barrel through...
My reaction time would be different.

HADLEY
I don't know what kind of bus it is,
alright?

LANE
Okay, fine. Let's recap; I'm crossing
the street, and here comes some kind
of bus, which may or may not be going
fast enough to hit me.

HADLEY
Yes...

LANE
Is it a double-long bus with that
accordion-type deal in the middle?

HADLEY
They're called articulated buses and
that for sure wouldn't matter.

LANE
I beg to differ. The additional length

                    LANE (CONT'D)
creates a radically different turning
radius, as well as a proportionately
different braking ratio. Not to
mention we haven't even considered
double decker buses, which are the
same length as a regular bus, but
twice as high as opposed to twice as
long.

                    HADLEY
A bus is a bus, Lane!

                    LANE
I think Rosa Parks would disagree!

                    HADLEY
Okay, you know what? Forget I asked,
you big, douchey douche face!

                    LANE
Whoa! Where did that come from?

                    HADLEY
You're impossible, that's where!

                    LANE
Don't get all up in my grill! If you
want me to wax hypothetical with you,
I need details!

                    HADLEY
It was a simple question! At least
it was supposed to be. Cheese and
crackers!

                    LANE
I have a vivid imagination, okay? And
I ride the bus. I'm pretty close to
it. Maybe it would be easier if it was
about someone else.

                    HADLEY
Fine, then. It's me. Okay? I'm
crossing the street. There's no
particular reason, the guy is just a
guy and the bus is any moving vehicle
with a steering wheel and four tires.

                    LANE
Oh, well that's easy, then. You get
plowed over and nobody calls for help
because your vague hypothetical has a
shocking lack of details. Case closed.

                    HADLEY
When the day comes that I snap and
kill you, they'll never find the body.

RIVALED

<u>INT. OFFICE - AFTERNOON</u>

GERRY IS SEATED WORKING. PAT STORMS IN,
FURIOUS.

            PAT
You are a filthy, cheating snake!

          GERRY
You're an evil, backstabbing,
conniving pig of a human being!

PAT IS COMPLETELY THROWN OFF.

            PAT
What? What the hell?! No, I'm not.
That's what you are.

          GERRY
I know. I just thought it would be fun
for you to know what it feels like to
be called that all the time. You can
get out of my office now.

            PAT
No... no! I will not be dismissed
out of hand like a... like... like
something no one wants anymore...

          GERRY
Newspaper delivery? The Post Office?
(THEN) Remakes of Spider-Man movies?

            PAT
You are insufferable! You know what
you did.

GERRY
I do. I took your client. I do not
apologize.

PAT
Poaching on each other's turf was
fine when we were flush, but times are
tough, Gerry. Not that many people can
afford feng shui consultants anymore.

GERRY
We live in Malibu, Pat. I feel I don't
need to further support the point.

PAT
Fine, we live in a bubble, but I need
to bring my percentages up. Shania is
axing everyone who isn't adding to
their roster. Give me back my client.

GERRY
My client.

PAT
Mine!

GERRY
Mine.

PAT
Mine! Mine! Mine!

GERRY
Wo de! That's Mandarin for 'mine'.
This could get boring quickly, so...

                    PAT
I knew you'd be this way about it.
(THEN) This is why I've already
damaged your car.

                    GERRY
What?! What the fuck is wrong with
you?

                    PAT
I'm desperate and I HATE you. I hate
you so much. Smashing your windshield
felt so good. It was hard for me stop
myself, but I did. I wanted to leave
room for us to negotiate.

                    GERRY
I'm not negotiating with you, you
fucking terrorist.

                    PAT
I think you are. I have compromising
Christmas party photos of you tagged
and ready to post on Facebook.

                    GERRY
I will delete your tag. I'll say the
pictures were photoshopped and you're
crazy, which you are.

                    PAT
I've poisoned your coffee this
morning. If you don't give me back my
client, I won't give you the antidote
and you'll die an excruciating death.

           GERRY
I don't believe that.

SCRAMBLING, PAT GRABS A PENCIL ON GERRY'S
DESK.

           PAT
I will stab you with this mechanical
pencil.

           GERRY
I don't believe that eith-

PAT STABS GERRY WITH THE PENCIL.

           GERRY (CONT'D)
Ow! Holy fuck! Fine, take back your
stupid client, you stupid nutjob.
(THEN) But you're paying for my new
windshield.

           PAT
Oh, I didn't actually do that. I
thought I'd mix up the things I'd
really do and really not do, to throw
your game off.

           GERRY
Stabbing me was on the list of "would
do"?

           PAT
I was just improvising at that point.
(THEN) So, I feel like we're good.

SNOWED

INT. DFW AIRPORT - 3 A.M.

JACE, A TICKET AGENT, ATTENDS TO A
DISAPPOINTED, BUT RESIGNED COUPLE. AS THEY
WALK OFF...

             JACE
    Thanks for your patience, folks!
    Air travel's not always a barrel of
    monkeys.

DALE MOVES UP IN LINE, COAT DRAPED OVER A
WHEELED CARRY-ON.

             DALE
    Hi there, (NOTICES NAME BADGE) uh....
    Jace. I need to check in and I know
    the weather is terrible, but please
    tell me my flight's not delayed.

             JACE
    Can I see your ID, please?

             DALE
    Sure.

DALE HANDS OVER A BOARDING PASS AND
DRIVER'S LICENSE. JACE TYPES INTO THE
COMPUTER.

             JACE
    Dale Feliciano... Okay, great news!
    All flights east are delayed because
    JFK's shut down due to an ice storm.

DALE

That is not great news! That's exactly
what I told you not to tell me.

JACE

The great news is that it's not just
your flight. That would be awful news.
Currently, everyone traveling across
America is in the same boat, so while,
generally speaking, that's bad news,
for you, or anyone in particular, it's
great news. They say misery loves
company... Bam! Silver lining!

DALE

Are you on anti-depressants?

JACE

Uh-huh, yes. It's a cocktail of
mood-enhancing pharmaceuticals that
stimulate my brain's neurotransmitters
and level out my dopamine. Isn't that
great news?

DALE

It's actually too much information.
Look, I have to get home to Brooklyn.
I know everyone here is saying the
same thing, but they're average,
stupid people with mediocre lives
who are just used to instant
gratification. Look at them swiping
away on their phones and drooling
at the Fox News Channel. They don't
really have to get home. They just
want to. I have to.

                    JACE
All lives matter.

                    DALE
You better watch who you say that
around. (THEN) Well, this is a pisser!

                    JACE
We can't control the weather, Dale.
May I call you Dale?

                    DALE
You just did. Look, Jace, since we're
on a first-name basis and all, I need
to get on the first flight out, as
soon as the weather lets up. Can you
make that happen?

                    JACE
We have thousands of travelers to
accommodate at this point. By and
large, we reroute passengers according
to their check-in time and you were...

CHECKS THE COMPUTER.

                    JACE (CONT'D)
...ah, last.

                    DALE
It figures. My Uber driver was a
moron. He spoke no English and he's
afraid to drive on the freeway, so
we took surface streets. I can tell
you where every H-E-B is from here to
downtown.

                    JACE
I don't mean this offensively, Dale,
but I really find that you New Yorkers
have a tendency to show up whenever
you want and expect to get whatever
you want. Is that what it's like
there? Is everyone aggressive and
cynical like you?

                    DALE
We just live life at a different pace,
Jace. People are people. I mean, I
never met anybody there like you,
but...

                    JACE
I've never been. I'm from New
Braunfels. It's between San Antonio
and Austin. I don't leave Texas for
personal reasons.

                    DALE
Uh-huh. (THEN) So, there's nothing you
can do?

                    JACE
Well, we do have a special
circumstance condition that might
help. Did somebody in your immediate
family die?

                    DALE
What? No.

                    JACE
Because if somebody in your immediate
family died, I could at least put you
at the top of the stand-by list and
possibly get you in a first-class seat
at no extra charge.

                    DALE
Oh, then yes. Somebody died. I just
got a text.

                    JACE
But you just said -

                    DALE
I was in denial. It's one of the seven
stages of grief. Another one is anger.
That's why I've been so hostile. But
I'm all done. I'm in acceptance now
and whatever the hell that last one is
- oh yeah, hope! I'm all hopeful.

                    JACE
I just need to know who: mother,
father, spouse, sibling...

                    DALE
All of them. They're all gone. It was
a big, freak mishap. I need to be at
the top of the list because my entire
family is very, very dead.

                    JACE
I'm so sorry for your loss. And to
find out in a text while you're at an

JACE (CONT'D)
airport away from home. Where are
people's manners?

DALE
Yeah, well... people are fucked. What
are you gonna do? Can you typity-type
me onto that list?

JACE
You should really think about
medication while you grieve.

DALE
I just need a new boarding pass,
thanks.

JACE
You know, if you combine Zoloft and
Xanax with an Adderall chaser, it
acts as a mood stabilizer, as well as
a mild hallucinogenic. Planning four
funerals is going to take a lot out of
you!

DALE
Noted. When can I leave?!

CHECKS COMPUTER.

JACE
Well, it looks like the storm is
dissipating and things are starting to
move again... right now, it looks like
I have something leaving at 8:30 p.m.,
from gate 11D... next Thursday.

                    DALE
THURSDAY?! That's four days away! What
about -

                    JACE
Your big fat lie? Sorry, city slicker,
we don't accommodate those. My advice
is to stay close by and check in at
the counter throughout the day.

                    DALE
Ah, crap! You have any extra pills??

                    JACE
I do not. Next!

Because it's hard for me to stop writing...

I hope you enjoyed the scenes! I always think of actors and writers as equal collaborators when it comes to realizing a character to its greatest potential. Assuredly, the writer starts off with a vision.

The characters that writers create do have parameters and definition. They aren't blank canvasses upon which actors can thrust their exploration and ideas beyond the guidelines. Characters exist to serve story. When actors recreate characters without regard to who they are on the page, they are, without realizing it, also rewriting the story.

Likewise, it takes the heart, soul, spirit, imagination and life experience of an actor to manifest a character into a believable human being who exists in the world. When actors round out a character's dialogue with intention and emotion, they have, together with the writer, created art and maybe magic.

My passion in life is to contribute magic to the world in whatever way possible. Art is subjective but we all know what feels good. Creating, imagining and discovering ourselves feels good. I'm sending this book into the world with a blessing: May the words I wrote bring permission to those who need it, a plot for those who lack one and a ripple of laughter that spreads deep and wide.

When I'm not in front of a computer writing, I'm at Actors Comedy Studio teaching. I'm biased, but it's the best place to study comedy acting in the world. (This is where others would quip, "Just kidding," "Of course, I own the place!" "LOL!" Nope, not doing that. I'm stone cold serious.)

And it's not because I'm an egomaniac. It's because there are too many wonderful people there with highly specialized skills not to feel that way. All the teachers and staff give their heart and invaluable information to the students freely. The students are kind, supportive of one another and career-minded professionals or learning to be. Everyone contributes to the success of each other and the idea that members of a community are stronger together as a whole.

And we learn how to win in a world-class city that barrels through the world like a runaway freight train that never slows down to let you hop on. I never stop learning. I'm a student there, too.

Acting is relatively easy when you know how. Auditioning for acting jobs and performing on camera in Hollywood is a whole other conversation. Actors Comedy Studio is where every aspect of building a career in comedy come together. I hope to see you there. In the meantime, feel free to reach out and say, "Hi!"